Avenyx's Sacrifice

By Lucas Delrose

For Jen,
You'll always be my harlot.
Love ya face!
~Lucas

Avenyx's Sacrifice

I've always found it remarkable how a name could accompany its owner so easily- whether it was one they wanted to keep, or one they did not particularly care for to begin with. I do not mean a given name received at birth or a family name passed down from generation to generation, but a title one earns or a label one is given. Take my title, for example, GOD. What is a God? What great deeds did I do to deserve this title? What makes me any different than any other?

A few things I suppose.

A very long time ago, back at the beginning of this world we call Thera, even before there were two moons in the night sky, I became part of a collective of people with unique gifts. Things were different back then. Many of the people who walked the land of Thera over the centuries that I have lived have had gifts. Gifts such as traveling at exceptional speeds, or turning into an animal in the blink of an eye, seeing or knowing what will happen before it has come to pass, or even *people who chose to study or become worldly in the magic arts. The gifts possessed by myself and the other members of our collective were far more advanced, and it is what we did with them that made us different from the rest. We were all drawn together to an undiscovered island in the middle of the great sea. Some came on great boats or on rafts they made themselves, while others used their gifts to travel to the island. Once we all arrived, we showed off our gifts, talents, and tricks to one another. It was then decided that we should use them to help the people of this world. We swore an oath, an oath that we would always do whatever we could to protect Thera itself and all its living creatures. We would never use our gifts to our advantage, never use them for evil or corruption, and above all, help those with similar gifts to understand and develop them.*

Before we went our separate ways to protect and watch over Thera, two of the collection offered us the gift of eternal life: a life without aging, a life without disease or sickness, and a life that could only be taken if slain or slaughtered. We decided it would be best if this gift was only shared between those of us who initially gathered together and it was agreed upon.

The title God did not come at once. We all achieved it differently, and each has a great tale of how we received it. I chose to wait a while before I shared my gifts with the people of Thera but once I began to use them, gradually over time, word got around of my deeds and abilities and the title of God was attached to my given name. At first, it was a blessing and a great honor. I felt proud that people looked up to me and believed in me. Over many, many years it was a title most of the 'Gods and Goddesses' found drew too much attention. Because of this, I made the decision to set out to find a quiet place to live a quiet life.

'God' or 'Goddess' is not the worst label that could have been given to us, but I still wonder, am I really a God? Was what I did that amazing, that world-changing? This question is something that has never left my mind and lurks there in the shadows. It makes me wonder how easily people name something - whether it's a name like 'God' that people look up to or one such as 'peasant' that people turn their nose and look down upon. It's just so remarkable how we often give someone or something a name without giving it a second thought, and how quickly it catches on, without anyone thinking, "Is this man really a God?"

Chapter 1

From high above the town center, perched on a rooftop like a hidden protector, lurking in the shadows, Avenyx looked over the silent main street, a dirt road down the center, lined with wooden building eerily still, in the shadows with no light to be seen. Shops now abandoned and boarded up, and those still running a functioning business, made the choice not to stay open after dark. This was not the town he once remembered, and all this changed seemed to happen in a short space of time. The town center Avenyx remembered was filled with so much life and entertainment. There was always some sort of late-night trade with shops still lit up and street lamps glowing. A lot of the time there was laughter and musical gatherings out on the street. Bands playing, people dancing, children playing and smiling faces. Almost certainly, great feasts were found spread over long tables and some of Ruby's finest brew to wash it down with. His heart was genuinely filled with sadness of a time almost forgotten. Although he often found solitude and peace in the silence. This was too silent, it was unsettled and made him wonder would a lively nightlife ever return to the town of Hazy Foot. Although it was what town folk called the dry season and the town was regularly somewhat empty of a nightlife, there was generally one or two intoxicated patrons staggering from Ruby's Tavern down the dirt strip that was the town center back to their homes. But some nights it was like no one lived there at all.

Hazy Foot was so named as it sat between the deadly, hazy swamp to the south and the foot of the large rocky mountain ranges in the north. It was a small secluded town, full of winding dirt roads, which aside from the road out of town, either lead to the town center or up into the mountains. Between the town center and the great mountain that constantly shadowed most of Hazy Foot, there were fields bordered by a massive swamp that enclosed the town. The empty fields were patches of dried-up grass that sporadically appeared across the hard, dirt soil. Wooden fence posts, some still standing, others lying lifeless on the ground, made up the borders between each property. The wire from the wired fences had been removed from most. People probably salvaged it up to make chicken coops or other projects. The homes themselves, left alone over time were rapidly deteriorating. Shattered glass windows, wooden doors blowing open in the wind, the exterior paintwork dried up and peeling. They just stood there lifeless, and slowly beginning to crumble into piles of ruin around the edges. Most were abandoned by those who left the town for one reason or another. The very few that remained inhabited were in slightly better condition. Some had trees or flowers growing close to the house. Or a barn or animal coop with very few animals roaming in them. Sadly, even still occupied, they looked like life had been sucked out of the old structures.

Hazy Foot had always been a humble town. Recent events had torn this once peaceful place apart, and many fled across the gloomy swamp, then the two days journey to the next town, in the hopes of finding a new place they could call home and start over. The once open and understanding community, so close-knit and always there for one another, had started singling out those who were different or, according to some, "tainted" and driving them out of the town. Still others fled in fear, whispers, and rumors of a contagious and terminal illness that had infected a handful of the townspeople, a disease known to most as 'Destined to Die'.

Avenyx thought about how it had all changed so quickly. He scolded himself constantly for being so distracted and petty over events in the past. Events that had kept him from being around as much and secluded himself from the town. How he wished things played out differently, he went through countless different scenarios in his head. He even thought about what would happen if he had never come to Hazy Foot at all, and stayed in a place where people would worship him and do his bidding. All in all, he did not realize that one simple act could turn a hero into a monster, changing people's opinions and starting a chain reaction that could last a lifetime with devastating results.

His train of thought was interrupted by voices and the sound of footsteps heading towards the deserted town center.

Avenyx, still hidden on the rooftop, watched curiously as an adolescent boy entered the town center. As the boy got closer to the rundown and boarded up bakery, Avenyx studied him, making out his features in the darkness. His exceptional night vision could make out Gaidence Valorgrace, it was the piercing blue eyes and just the way he held himself when walked, so upright and proper even though he seemed a little rushed or in a panic. Then Avenyx noticed why he may seem rushed as he could also make out the flames from roaring torches heading from the same direction.

The boy approached quickly, trying to hide in the shadows slipping down the side alley unnoticed. He planned to find safety from his pursuers. Avenyx could hear his panting breath and could see the look of panic as his eyes darted around quickly.

As the light of the flames drew near, Avenyx could make out three boys in their late teens, around the same age as Gaidence. He tried to study their faces but could not recognize the youths, it was harder for him to be so separated from the younger generation. As they made their way towards the side alley, they began to speak. The voices did sound familiar to him, a friend of Gaidence's he was almost certain, but sometimes friendships don't last... The boy's name had escaped Avenyx's memory but he recalled the two boys laughing and joking together some time ago.

"There is no point in running Gaidence Valorgrace! We're going to catch you and you're going to tell us where we can find him! Even if we need to beat it out of you."

Avenyx knew of Gaidence and his family very well. Although he had never spoken to the teen, he had watched him grow up from a distance or unseen. Gaidence had grown into a sensible and well-respected young man. Avenyx remembered the time Gaidence was caught kissing Melinda on the night of the annual double eclipse festival, behind the giant apple tree just outside of town. He also remembered more recently seeing him trying hard to hold back the tears, as he sat by the edge of the swamp when Melinda and her family moved away. Melinda was special, she had a gift that could make flowers bloom from buds before your very eyes, and this was one of the things Gaidence liked so much about her. However, being different was no longer something everyone accepted. This is one of the reasons why Avenyx chose to watch from afar and only intervene when needed.

Watching over the town and its people at night was something that Avenyx had become accustomed to. The night was always his favorite time when the moons and stars were high above and darkness fell. He rarely came out during the day, and if he did it would be to stock up on supplies then disappear so he could continue getting by unnoticed. The very few that believed Avenyx was still around, did not share it with the others. He wanted most to believe he was gone, driven out by those who turned against him on that most dreadful night. The night that Avenyx would always remember, regret, and blame himself for. If only he had known someone had been watching him, waiting for him to make one little error, so they could use it for their evil-doing, which would last a very long time.

The trio had made their way to the side alley, peering through the gaps in the wooden boards against the windows to see if Gaidence had crept in and hidden inside.

"He wouldn't have gone in there," the one Avenyx assumed to be the leader called. He seemed more determined and bossier than the other two. "He might be thin but he wouldn't fit through those gaps. Down the alley, I bet."

In the shadows above, Avenyx used the cover of night to keep himself hidden and his keen night vision to keep an eye on things. His black tailored suit made the perfect camouflage as he crept along the rooftop for a closer look. Silently he stood looking down at the three boys edging further in the alley. From his position he could also make out Gaidence down the end with no escape, crouching behind a large wooden crate. Knowing Gaidence was outnumbered, he feared what these boys might do to him. Avenyx could have simply watched on, but he knew this was more than just some boys having a bit of fun. This was dangerous, Avenyx was left with no choice but to intervene.

He lifted his grey eyes to the night sky, then raised his hands high above his head and whispered a chant to the darkness. As if from nowhere, a thick, black mist formed in the alley, making it impossible for the boys to see more than a few steps in front of them.

"Where did this mist come from?" Called a stocky boy with fear in his voice. His eyes darted around quickly to find the culprit.

"Just get down there and bring me Gaidence," the leader ordered, giving the other a shove into the darkness.

"Eventide! Extinguish that flame!" Avenyx's deep voice boomed from above. As the boy holding the torch gazed up to search where the voice had come from, a black raven swooped down from the darkness and knocked the torch to the ground. The flame went out. Avenyx knew it was time to teach these boys a lesson and even up the numbers. He leaped down from the roof above into the thick black mist. It was as if he was gliding down with his black cape flowing behind until he was safely on the ground, surrounded in darkness.

"Stay down Gaidence," he whispered over his broad shoulder, and the magic of the fog took the message to Gaidence, who had crouched and hidden at the end of the alley. Avenyx used his advanced sight and enhanced hearing to listen to the oncoming stranger entering the mist. He could make out his image slowly coming closer. He could hear the sound of the boy's footsteps as his boots pressed down on the dirt with every step he took and the scraping every time he lifted his feet to take another. Avenyx waited patiently, knowing just a few more steps and the boy was in his range.

"Have you got him yet?" Avenyx heard the leader call smugly, standing on the outside of the mist.

The thug inside the mist took another step closer towards Avenyx, unaware he was waiting for him. Suddenly the thug froze. He realized he was not alone in the darkness. Without his gang to back him up, he might not be able to take on the unknown presence.

Avenyx took his opportunity. He tightened his grip on his long black cane then swung it swiftly, striking the boy on the back of the legs. The boy's legs buckled before him, but before he had the chance to yell out in pain or hit the floor, Avenyx caught him, dropped his cane, and placed his hand tightly around his mouth to prevent him from calling out.

"What's going on in there?" Another call came from outside the fog.

The boy began to struggle in Avenyx's arms.

Avenyx tilted his head down. His shoulder-length silky black hair draped across the terrified teen's face. His round brown eyes were filled with fear and terror as he glanced up into Avenyx's menacing eyes. Avenyx moved his head closer now, so close his lips were almost touching the boy's ear as he whispered, "By the night, I send you to sleep."

As the placated teen's eyes began to flutter, Avenyx continued softly, "dream of me." He smiled, watching as the boy's eyes closed, falling instantly into a deep sleep.

Avenyx removed his hand from the boy's mouth, laid him on the ground, and picked up his cane.

On the outside of the mist, straining their eyes to peer into the darkness, the remaining two boys stood.

"I suggest you leave now and return in the morning to collect your friend. Young Gaidence does not deserve to be chased and bullied any longer." Avenyx's voice roared from inside the darkness.

Both boys froze instantly until the leader took charge again and shoved his friend forward towards the mist.

"You want to prove yourself to him? To join them? We need to get him a *tainted*. So get in there!" The leader ordered, giving his friend another shove.

Hesitantly, the younger boy inched closer toward the mist. He took a deep breath and turned back to his friend who just stood there glaring at him. Then he made his way in. He wasn't in there too long before he came straight back out.

"Well?"

"I'm kind of scared of the dark," he replied standing at the edge of the mist with his back to it.

Suddenly, from the mist came a gloved hand which wrapped itself around the boy's mouth and dragged him in. The leader watched in horror, too scared to run away. He knew he had to do this. He had to prove himself. Gaidence knew where the tainted was hiding and if he got hold of Kendall, he would be accepted. With this thought, he built up enough courage to speak.

"I'll find him, Gade! There isn't a hiding place in this town that I don't know. He's tainted and things are changing. We don't want tainted in our world anymore. Thera will be pure! He... we will make it happen, you will see." With that, he ran out of the town center and into the night.

The mist began to clear and Avenyx stood tall with the two thugs laid unconscious at his feet and their arms at their sides.

"It's safe now, Gaidence, you may come out of hiding," Avenyx called.

Slowly the adolescent boy rose from his hiding spot. He pushed back the fringe of mousy brown hair covering his face, returning it to a straight, even part. He began to brush the dust from his clean shaven face, leaving dust smudged under his nose, where the tiny stubble of a mustache was trying to push its way through. He then dusted off his button-up navy shirt and black slacks, which had been torn at the right knee during his eventful evening.

"Thank you," Gaidence said, trying to sound confident. Although generally quietly spoken, he always spoke clearly and politely.

"You are most welcome," Avenyx replied and bowed his head low to Gaidence.

Avenyx could tell Gaidence was a little surprised and possibly curious as he inspected the boys laying on the ground. His blue inquisitive eyes changed to what Avenyx sensed as fear or confusion as he looked up to Avenyx.

"They are perfectly fine. They may have a little bruising and pain in the morning but they are just asleep."

"You came to my rescue. I hope one day I can repay you."

Avenyx chuckled, pleased with the boy's chivalry.

"Oh, that will not be necessary. I generally don't need rescuing. I do have a few gifts that aid me in escaping most situations."A genuine smile came over Avenyx's face and he could not recall the last time someone had assumed he needed rescuing.

Gaidence took a step back and was a little afraid, "you made the darkness come?" he asked. Gaidence had heard stories about the one who can control darkness, one who once protected and watched over the town. He studied Avenyx's face a little, trying to picture him. It was only a small town and he was certain he had seen him before once or twice. Yes, Gaidence was now sure he had seen him a long time ago. Although he appeared to be just a normal man, how did he save him from three boys?

"Yes, that was I."

"Are you…" Gaidence began to ask but could not find the right words to say. His voice froze in his throat.

"Yes, yes I am. My name is Avenyx, also known as the God of Night."Gaidence slowly took a step forward and extended his arm, while putting his hand out to shake the God's. His hand trembled a little as he did. Avenyx's first instinct was to take a step back, but taking a back step was something he'd done for far too long. He looked Gaidence in the eyes and raised his own hand. With a firm grip, he shook it. "Now then, why were you being chased by those boys Gaidence?"

"How do you know my name?"

"Do you often answer a question with a question of your own?"

"Yes. No! I'm just, well it's just.... you look so normal."

Avenyx smiled and shook his head. "You expected something more?"

Gaidence didn't know how to respond, so he just shrugged his shoulders.

"We Gods are all quite... normal as you put it. I'm sure you know a few other gifted people in this town. Gods and goddesses are simply gifted with a few extra talents. Avenyx will be quite sufficient. Please, don't call me by my title--sir, or mister, or God. We're given names for a reason. Now, if you would kindly answer my question, I will happily answer yours."

"Yes, sir--I mean Avenyx."

Avenyx shook his head and grinned. There was no doubt about it. Gaidence was truly a Valorgrace, just like his father. Their politeness was always so genuine, and it warmed Avenyx's heart.

"Those boys are desperate to join a new crusade that has arisen, and eager to prove themselves. I'm sure you have noticed it dividing the town. They don't seem to like people who are different. Some women won't trade with others, as rumor has it, they have a gifted husband, or a brother with abilities, or daughter. Something really needs to be done, before it gets any worse. Some won't even leave their homes! If they do, it's to pack up and leave the town altogether." Gaidence passionately explained.

"Different? Are we not all different in our ways? Is it not what makes us unique?"

"Yes. Different like you--gifted I think you referred to it as."

"So, they are non-believers."

"They are. However, it is much more than that. They wish to force out anyone gifted. Witches, Sorcerers, Shifters, Arcons, Prophets, Mind Readers…"

"I understand what you mean, Gaidence Valorgrace. This brings me once again to my original question. Why are they chasing you?"

Avenyx looked down at Gaidence waiting for an answer. He knew Gaidence was stalling as he kicked rocks in the dirt. It was as if Avenyx could see his mind ticking over, thinking of how to reply to the question that he did not want to give an answer to. "I do not mean any offense and it certainly was an honor to meet you. I have always been a believer in the Gods and often wondered if the great God of Night was still around watching us. I really must head off. I need to check on my brother and make sure he is safe."

"Of course," Avenyx nodded, putting the pieces together in his head. Avenyx was a smart man, and not much slipped by him. He did not want to pressure Gaidence, but he needed to know more.

"How is little Kendall? He would be growing up so fast, seven years younger than you would mean he has seen 12 double eclipses?"

"Yes... how do you know of my brother?"

"How about I accompany you back to check on your brother and we answer each other's questions along the way?"

"I wouldn't want to burden you any further. You have taken care of the other two, and I can outrun Jacobus if we cross paths again tonight."

"That was Jacobus?" Avenyx's finally recalling the third boy's family. "He has put on a little weight. His mother's pumpkin pie always was divine," Avenyx grinned to himself as he remembered Jacobus' mother, Glendell - such a sweet, plumpish woman who loved to cook, and loved to eat what she cooked just as much. Her pumpkin pies were her signature dish. She would bring them to every town event and although Avenyx contemplated a second piece every time she offered, he always politely declined. He was a firm believer in not overindulging when it came to food. In his travels, he'd seen places where food such as pumpkin pie was a rarity, and wanted to make sure everyone got their fair share. He knew Glendell always had plenty for a second piece but just those memories of places in poorer conditions stuck with him. That and knowing what making a habit of taking a second piece would do to his slender figure.

"Accompanying you would not be a burden at all and honestly, I am curious. I would like to know more about this crusade and why Jacobus would be chasing you. As I recall, the two of you were friends."

Gaidence gave Avenyx an unsure look. He wondered how he knew so much about him and where he had come from. His mother used to remind him when he was young, never to ask questions about the Gods and Goddesses of this world, for this was just how it was. Sadly, nowadays his mother was no longer around. When she had been she would pray to the Gods, many times a day. It would always be to protect and watch over her two boys. Gaidence smiled to himself. He knew her prayers were being answered. How he wished to see her again one day and tell her. Although he was a little disappointed. From the stories he was told when he was younger, he had expected some great, shiny being. Instead, he was standing in front of an average looking man, a little darker, and more mysterious with his black attire. Avenyx still looked so full of life for someone who had been around so long. His hair was black and long, so clean and shiny. He had silver eyes, although they didn't look aged; you know they'd seen many things. His tailored suit covered this arms and legs, but Gaidence could tell he was very toned, as the sleeves of his jacket sat tight around his biceps. His face was pale, which Gaidence would expect for one who prefers the night. He was also taller than Gaidence imagined. Gaidence considered himself an average height, he knew Avenyx was easily over six feet. Gaidence thought it would be in his best interest to let Avenyx accompany him, and he could learn so much more about the world he didn't know. He'd always been curious about what life was like on the other side of the swamp that separated Hazy Foot from everything else. What were the people like? Did they have different homes? Or different foods? And then there were the tales his mother used to tell him. Marnie had never traveled beyond the swamp herself, but she always hoped to one day. He remembered when she would talk to people at the markets who had come from somewhere else. She'd come home and tell the boys of the adventures she'd heard. Then there were the books. She didn't own many herself, but she would borrow them from different people in the town and sometimes read them to Gaidence and Kendall. She had the spirit of an Adventurer, his father would always say, and Gaidence believed that part of it was in him too, until he became the sole caregiver for his brother. "It would be an honor to have you accompany me."

"Then you are most welcome. However, there is one more who shall join us."

Gaidence gave Avenyx an odd look as Avenyx raised his right arm, extending it out to the side.

"Eventide! Return to me!" Avenyx called into the night. Gaidence gazed up at the twinkling dark sky where the two moons sat side by side. He could hear a noise that sounded like the flapping of wings. From the darkness, a large black bird swooped in and landed on Avenyx's arm, then made its way to his shoulder to perch.

"Allow me to introduce to you my companion. This is Eventide the raven."

Gaidence stared into the bird's dark black eyes, amazed at how well trained it was.

"Shall we then?" Avenyx said pointing his cane in the direction that led out of the alley.

Chapter 2

Avenyx and Gaidence walked along the dirt road that led away from the town center with Eventide circling above. The road was lined with purple wildflowers, the same that grew on either side of the few roads running through the town. Although the flowers were barely visible in the darkness, they were one of the things about the town that never changed, since they always bloomed no matter the season.

The night was dark and quiet, most were safely in their homes. Even Ruby's Tavern closed earlier each night lately, except every 4th full moon when the workers came home from working up in the mountains. The street lanterns, which were once lit every night, also remained dark. The posts they stood upon were just that; posts, standing empty in the darkness, the candles lifeless and unlit.

As they walked, Avenyx thought to himself how quickly things in the town had changed, how families had just got up and moved away. He found it odd, then realized he had not been paying enough attention to notice this sooner. He knew something had changed but couldn't quite put his finger on it, and hadn't cared enough to investigate further. He told himself not to get involved in the town again, not after last time, but now he knew he could not live like this any longer. Something was afoot and if the gods didn't step in, the town he loved so much would be changed forever, or worse- destroyed by hate, or this crusade that seemed to be dividing them.

"I feel it's only fair I respond to your question," Avenyx spoke, then smiled, looking down at Gaidence. "Many moons ago, around the time you were born, I was around a lot more, rather than lurking from the shadows at night. Being such a close-knit community, as most small towns are, we all knew one another and quite well. Although I rarely came out during the day, I did often head down to Ruby's regularly at night. We all used to drink, unwind, laugh, and have a good time. Some nights it would get rowdy, maybe a little too much drinking, chairs getting broken. Ruby herself on occasion would tip buckets of ice water over patron's heads telling them to leave and cool off. Once or twice I personally witnessed Ruby literally throwing a man through the doors out on the street. She's a fine Tavern

Owner, our Ruby. It was always a good time at Ruby's. Sadly, ten eclipses ago, or years as we now call them, that all changed and I became solitary. I hid away in the mountains, sneaking into town only when I needed supplies. I could not grow or farm on my own."

Gaidence had a massive grin on his face, listening to Avenyx reminisce. He liked to listen to tales and stories of the old days. It was not often he heard them now, mainly when he came to the town center to trade. But that was just conversations he overheard. It was nice to have someone actually tell them to him. "I have small memories of when Ruby's was open regularly at night. When the workers, including my father, would visit it regularly. My mother would often send me to go collect him."

The mention of Gaidence's father piqued a memory in Avenyx, "Ticcarus Valorgrace. A man who could always make you smile, always had a tale to tell, and was always ready for any adventure. It's a shame he never got the chance to have one. He was such a kind-hearted man. I'm deeply sorry for your loss Gaidence, I only wish you had the chance to know him as well as I did."

"Thank you. People do often mention stories of him. He was a remarkable man."

"And that he was. The older ones in this town remember me, although ever since a terrible incident I believe the town has been quite torn. Some feel their

God had let them down." Avenyx's voice trailed off as he spoke.

"You mean the fires?" Gaidence asked and as soon as the words left his lips, he wished he could take them back.

"It is a topic I do not wish to discuss," Avenyx quickly snapped back.

"I'm sorry, sir."

Avenyx realized his harsh change towards Gaidence, it had been a while since he'd had this much interaction with another person, he knew he may have overreacted. "You need not apologize. I do miss the days that have now passed; I must visit dear Ruby again soon. Such a sweet woman with the kindest heart. I miss her greatly. I am not surprised she is one of the only places in this town that still remains. She would never give up on this town, such a stubborn woman."

"I find it strange I have not seen you or recognized you. I've not even heard a mention of you in quite some time now."

"The people in this town have changed. When I do come out to check on the town, it is usually at night and I do it unnoticed. I intervene when I need to, like tonight for example. Things also change, our world moves on quickly but at the same time, it doesn't stray too far from where it is at... I apologize, I might not be making much sense."

"I think our world moves quite fast and we grow rather quickly."

Avenyx smiled.

"I suppose you would, although it works a little differently for me I'm afraid. When you've lived as long as I have, and watched people grow old while you do not, it all seems so different."

Gaidence glanced up at his tall, dark, and mysterious hero. He didn't appear to be getting older. Maybe a little older than himself it would seem, certainly younger than his father was before he died.

"So how old are you?" Gaidence asked, intrigued.

"I wish I had an answer for you young man, sadly I do not know. Gods and Goddesses do not add another year to our age each time the two moons eclipse in the night sky. Some say we have been around so long we have forgotten. It's bound to happen after living so long, you forget things that have happened in the past. I tend to think an immortal does not age, so we should not really have one."

"What if you had to take a guess?"

"Guessing generally assumes one has not put enough thought into the matter and comes up with an answer which is irrelevant."

"Well, what if you thought about it?"

"Young Gaidence, this topic of conversation is not going anywhere and you will not get the answers you seek." Avenyx narrowed his eyes at Gaidence and raised his brows.

"You're rather interesting and different from what I expected you to be. I like how you talk... your sentences. And how you call me 'Young Gaidence' when I'm practically a man, who would be sent to work in the mountains if it wasn't just me and Kendall."

"And you *Gaidence Valorgrace* seem to talk quite a lot."

There was silence between the duo for a brief moment.

"I'm...sorry. It's...just that..." Gaidence stammered not sure what to say. He did not mean to upset Avenyx, or seem intrusive in any way. He was quite surprised how easy talking to Avenyx actually was. To Gaidence, he did not seem like some great higher being. He did not seem any better than Gaidence, or Jacobus, or anyone for that matter. To Gaidence, he seemed an equal. He knew it was one of the Gods, the beings he looked up to and prayed to in desperate times. However, getting to know him, Gaidence felt that everyone was different, and we should just treat them equally. So why should he treat Avenyx any differently just because of the title he'd been given. It was not that Gaidence didn't respect him, or believe in him. He just felt comfortable talking to him.

A smile slowly crept across Avenyx's face, and he placed his hand on Gaidence's shoulder.

"I do not need an apology or explanation," Avenyx said.

"I'm really grateful you offered to walk with me."

"It has been a great learning experience for us both."

"Yes, I agree. We're just about there, I'm heading in that direction," Gaidence said, as he pointed into an almost empty field. In the field, Avenyx could make out what looked like a tiny abandoned chicken coop, or at least it once was.

"Do you not trust me Gaidence? I believe that is not your home."

"It's not that at all. My brother Kendall is someplace else. I meet him here. It's the safest way so Jacobus does not find him. Kendall believes Jacobus wishes to take him as a captive to the man behind this crusade."

"Kendall is different, isn't he Gaidence?"

Gaidence stopped walking and slowly took in a deep breath, tears began to form in his eyes.

"I won't let them get him Avenyx. He's not tainted. Tainted is such a nasty word to use, what he has is a gift. He doesn't want to hurt anyone with it, and I can't see how he could. My mother said the Gods only give these gifts to good-hearted people. Those who will use them for good. He's my little brother, he wouldn't hurt anybody. All the things Jacobus has been saying and now others…"

"What are they saying?"

"It's not important, I know it's lies. Kendall told me it wouldn't get better though. He said this was the start of something major, he was scared. I didn't want to believe him, I still don't want to. I told him I didn't want to hear anymore, but he has no one to talk to and he just seems so afraid."

"Does your brother know things that are going to happen before they do?" Avenyx asked.

Gaidence was not able to hold the tears back any longer and a couple rolled down his face. He tried to be strong but his brother was his weakness. He did not respond, just nodded.

"Would you like me to talk to Kendall? I am happy to help."

Gaidence shook his head as he wiped the tears from his face.

"I feel I have told you too much already," he sighed, "my brother does not wish for others to know, as too many already do. Because of this, he is being hunted."

"I can offer protection."

"You have been so generous and offered too much already. I am truly grateful but he is my brother and I will protect him."

"Although I do not agree with your decision, I respect your wishes. You are as noble as your father was. Eventide will accompany you until you are with your brother. When you reach him, dismiss Eventide by saying 'Eventide, return home.'"

Avenyx turned his head to face the raven, whispered to it, and the bird spread its big black wings and continued to patrol the area just above their heads.

"I am truly grateful and in your debt. I promise you I will return the favor one day," Gaidence said, bowing to Avenyx.

"One final token?" Avenyx asked and reached into his black coat pocket, removing a shiny black stone. He held it out in the palm offering it to Gaidence. "Take it, boy." Hesitantly, Gaidence did as the God requested and took the polished piece of rock. It looked like it was some sort of gemstone, but none that Gaidence had ever seen. It was smooth to touch as he ran his fingers over it. He felt what he thought were dents or chips in it, but as he drew it closer to his face, he realized they were carvings--three little stars sculpted into the stone. In the daylight, Gaidence imagined the stone would look like the night sky, with the stars twinkling. Gaidence knew this symbol well; it represented the God of Night. His mother would sew and embroider it into different clothing and rugs she would make. Gaidence looked back up at Avenyx, curious about the offering he had just been given, but before he could ask, the question was answered.

"It's called a God Stone. I do not feel comfortable with its title, however, this is what it is known as. It is mine, in fact. If you shatter it, I will know you are in trouble and do anything in my power to aid you."

"I can't," Gaidence said politely and tried to hand it back.

"Please. If your brother says this is only the beginning, then I fear you may need it. This is a simple gesture, and if people are grouping against you, chasing you at night, you may need all the allies you can get."

Gaidence quickly shoved the stone in his pocket. He created a fist with his right hand and placed it against his chest over his heart, then he looked up at Avenyx and smiled. "By the Gods," he said.

Avenyx smiled. It was a gesture he had not seen in some time, and it warmed his heart. A simple friendly gesture, one that believers in the Gods would make, to wish one another a successful journey along whatever path they were about to take or until they met again. It was a reminder that the Gods would watch over them. Avenyx thought it was a silly tradition, but he did feel respected when people would use it towards him. To show his gratitude he lifted his right hand, made a fist, and placed it against his own chest. "By the Gods, Gaidence Valorgrace."

With that Gaidence departed, running off into the field with Eventide following above. Avenyx looked on for a moment, tempted to follow but knew that this was against the boy's wishes. *Too long I have kept my distance from this town; this must change,* Avenyx thought to himself, before disappearing into the night.

A young boy with short, messy, blonde hair frantically ran through an empty pumpkin field. He turned his head constantly, looking in every direction to make sure he was not being followed. In the distance, he spied his destination. It was a small, deserted barn next to the remains of a home that had been burnt to rubble a long time ago. He panted, gasping for air, but did not stop running until he made it safely to the barn. Once there he crawled through a small opening near the bottom corner of the large, bolted barn door. The barn was pitch black. The boy did not bother to adjust his eyes to the darkness, as he knew it was just too dark and he wouldn't be able to make out anything clearly anyway. Although he couldn't see, he knew he was not alone. He slowly rose to his feet, edging with tiny side steps along the barn wall. He kept his back pressed up against the wall the entire time so he would not trip over or run into the other person.

"Have you eaten?" The soft voice of a woman spoke.

"Yes ma'am," Kendall's soft and timid voice replied.

"Are you telling me the truth now?"

"Yes ma'am, I honestly have."

"Probably not enough."

Kendall sensed the woman move closer by the scent of her perfume, the smell of fresh flowers. It reminded him of his mother, who would often take him on walks around the town. They would pick flowers together, then arrange them in baskets at home to take to town on the first day of the new moon for trade.

The woman was close now. She held out her hand to give something to Kendall. He reached out, searching for her hand in the darkness, and took what she was holding. It felt smooth and round. He smiled and knew it was a shiny red apple. He had never seen this woman's face, and there was no routine or guarantee she would be there, but when she was, sometimes she brought offerings. On cold nights, she brought a woven rug. They would sit together, either in silence or she would tell him tales/stories. She spoke of other gifted people she knew, or once knew in the town. She spoke how many moved on through the swamp and across a great field to the next town. She spoke knowledgeably, but only in small amounts, of a great disease that affected very few in the town. It would turn their blood black at an instant, and eventually kill them. She assured him not many caught this, but people left in fear of it. Most often she spoke of a God; a God that once protected the town. Whether they sat for a long period or a brief sitting, they very much enjoyed each other's company. As much as Kendall enjoyed listening to the stranger, he felt she enjoyed talking to him just the same. He trusted her and felt a strange connection with her. He smiled, thinking about this as he took a bite into the juicy apple.

"Why do you run and hide? Why do you not stand up to them?"

"I am but a boy. Their numbers may be only a few now, but in time they will become many. Wouldn't you run and hide if the people you once thought were friends turned against you?"

There was now silence for quite some time, besides the crunching of Kendall eating his apple.

"Then why don't you come with me? I will protect you."

"I do not want to burden, lady. You are very kind; however, I feel something troubles and pains you. A pain that you one day wish to settle by whatever means and I would just get in your way, distract you from doing what you feel you should."

"You know many things, but you still run."

"I feel we both know one can't run forever, prey eventually gets caught. Prey can't keep repeating the same habits expecting safety, it always lets its guard down, even if it's just for a brief moment, and then their pursuer has them. Once I have been captured--a fate that draws closer every time the moons rise--it will all begin. A beginning that sets the rest in motion."

"And how do you know of this?"

Although they had this same conversation before, each time it ends the same, and the woman never gets her answer.

"I must meet with my brother," Kendall said, as he quickly crawled back under the gap of the wooden door. He glanced around, making sure once again that no one was watching, then darted back into the night.

<u>Chapter 3</u>

A full day had passed since Avenyx's meeting with Gaidence. Avenyx had thought long and hard, trying to piece together the missing details. As hard as he tried there was still so much he could not figure out. He had many questions he still needed answers for and he also knew there was one person who would give them to him.

The old wooden tavern doors squeaked with signs of deterioration as Avenyx swung them open. They continued to sway back and forth slowly, until they came to a stop again in the center as he entered the gloomy, low-lit tavern. He stood tall in the doorway, the darkness of the night sky and stars twinkling in the background against it. He glanced around for a moment, expecting there to be more people quenching their thirst on such a warm evening. Also, it was the first night of the workers returning home for their three-day break from laboring up in the mountains, but Ruby's

Tavern was deserted. Although surprised, Avenyx was happier that it was like this. He did not wish to make a huge scene as he was here with a purpose. Renowned for its special whiskey and friendly atmosphere, Ruby's was also a place he could go for information. Nothing went on in the town without Ruby knowing about it. In the earlier days, once the people of the town had a few too many drinks, their lips got loose and their secrets would slip out. In recent times, people confided in Ruby and came to her for advice, so she still knew all the ins and outs of Hazy Foot.

As Avenyx made his way across the large room towards the bar, his eyes darted around, trying to find the woman he was seeking. Once he reached the bar, he pulled up a wooden stool and sat, waiting to be attended to.

The bar ran the full length of the left-hand side of the establishment. Behind the bar, the wall was filled with a range of different shaped bottles and glasses. Most bottles were half full or contained some sort of liquid in them, whether it be whiskey, soda, or some other kind of beverage. Each glass or bottle on the shelves behind the bar was crystal clear, almost sparkling. Not a speck of dust could be spotted in the entire place. Avenyx's side of the bar was lined with bar stools, evenly spaced. As he continued to look around the room, he did notice the spot in the darkened back corner near the staircase, where he used to always sit, was now empty. Avenyx's favorite feature of the tavern was the grand staircase. Upon it laid a red carpet that led to the second floor where the bedrooms were (Ruby had been known on occasion to lease these out, or let her workers stay in them while they earned their keep working for her). The stairs were lit by big red lanterns, that matched the red curtains at each of the tavern's windows, and the red candles that burned at every table. Each table also had a freshly-picked flower next to the candle, providing a sweet aroma. Avenyx often thought it was amazing that Ruby, being named after a red precious gem, had themed everything to match the beautiful stone, from the look of her tavern to her own appearance.

Avenyx turned to the barman, who had made his way over to him. He stood tall, with his brown hair neatly kept. He wore a crisp white shirt, black slacks, and a red bowtie that sat a little crooked around his neck. He smiled as he greeted Avenyx, and Avenyx returned the smile. Avenyx noticed a deep scar on the right-hand side of the young man's face. In his hand, the barman carried a damp cloth he had been cleaning the bar with when Avenyx entered. He was sure Ruby had him clean it every day so it was always spotless. The barman looked at Avenyx, puzzled for a moment, then a look of surprise spread across his face and he could no longer keep eye contact with Avenyx. Instead, he glanced past him nervously.

"Good evening sir, may I interest you in a cold beverage on this warm night?" The barman said, rather quickly, and in a timid, almost frightened, and nervous voice.

"Thank you. I would like--" Avenyx began, but was cut off by the raised voice of an elderly woman who called from the top of the staircase. Although her voice was aged it still was powerful and had such authority in it.

"In a tall glass, three quarters tonic water, two squeezes of lemon, three cubes of ice and the tiniest hint of sweetening syrup. If it's not too much of an inconvenience I will be extremely grateful, thank you."

Avenyx and the barman both instantly turned their heads to the top of the staircase. Avenyx knew very well there was only one person who knew exactly what he liked to drink, and how he ordered it. As they looked up, the elderly woman gracefully made her way down the staircase. She was elegantly dressed in a bright red gown made from the finest of silks. The trimming at the bottom and around the top of the neck of the gown was edged with black lace. The neckline came down in a V and prominently on her chest she wore a dainty gold necklace with a ruby shining brightly on it--her most proud possession. Almost no Therian wore gold, as it was far too rare; most of the time if someone did wear gold it had been given to them as a gift. A gift from a God or Goddess.

Avenyx looked up at her face and smiled. The woman also wore a smile across her aged and wrinkled face. She wore bright red lipstick across her lined lips, and her white hair was up in curls. Avenyx stared, admiring her beauty. He'd known as soon as he heard the voice who it belonged to. She was an old friend who he had not seen in some time and missed greatly. As she approached, he stood and bowed his head to the woman.

"Off you go then and get this thirsty man a drink. I would like an orange juice, also, my dear," she ordered the barman, who rushed off at her demand. The elderly woman then stood in front of Avenyx and looked him up and down as he held his position still bowing his head.

"Haven't aged a day," she said as she shook her head. "Come now! Stop that, you and your politeness and manners. I should be the one bowing at you, you are a God after all. I am just a simple, humble, and now old, tavern owner. Come now Avey, take your seat."

Avenyx lifted his head and waited for the woman to pull up a stool and take a seat. My dearest Ruby, I am delighted to see you once again," Avenyx said, raising his hand and extending it to Ruby. Ruby placed her wrinkled hand into his; he took hold of it, lifted to his lips, and softly kissed it.

"It's been far too long, Avey. So, what brings you here after all this time? You may have noticed things

40

aren't as busy as they once were," she said glancing around, he could sense the disappointment in her tone.

"Can an old friend not visit unannounced?"

"Not this old friend. There is always a method in your madness. I may be old Avey, but I haven't lost my marbles yet."

"Oh Ruby, I have not the slightest idea of your meaning." Avenyx was trying to be subtle. He knew he had not seen Ruby in a long time, and he should have visited more often. Valid reasons kept him away from Ruby's as well as the town. He needed to know what had happen in his absence, but now he felt guilty that he had come to see Ruby out of the blue after so long, simply because he wanted information from her.

"Come out with it before the sun rises."

He hesitated a moment, about to blurt it out, but was saved by the barman returning with the drinks. He placed the drinks on the bar in front of them and stood there for a moment as Avenyx pulled out a leather coin pouch from under his cape. He removed four small bronze-colored coins and handed them to the barman.

"This is more than enough for the drinks sir," he said, beginning to hand half the coins back.

"The rest is for yourself, I'm sure they will come in handy." Avenyx smiled.

"I pay him a fair wage, I'll have you know," Ruby muttered.

"I'm sure you do, however, I'm giving him a little extra."

"Would there be anything else?" The barman added, with a large grin across his face.

"That will be all for now, thank you for your service." Avenyx smiled back. The barman began to walk off, then turned back. "I prayed one day you would return to us and protect us again. I knew you had not abandoned us, as most have said." The barman made a fist with his right hand and placed it on his chest. "By the Gods," he whispered and hurried off into the back room behind the bar.

Avenyx watched him wander off, speechless. He wanted to know more about what people had been saying about him abandoning them. He wanted to know who these people were spreading such tales. By the time he found his voice it was too late, as the barman was out of sight. He turned to Ruby, who could read the expression of confusion on his face. She looked back at him blankly and he shook his head, changing the subject.

"I spoke with Gaidence Valorgrace last night. My, how Ticcarus's oldest boy has grown. He would be so proud if he was still with us today," Avenyx said.

"Yes that he would have. I see the boys in town now and then, doing so well after all the tragedy they have faced."

"He told me some things, Ruby. Some rather unsettling things about the town and the people I thought I once knew."

"I think we need to have a talk alone. I feel there is a lot I need to fill you in on and this may not be the place for it." Ruby said, glancing her eyes unsurely around the room. He shook his head and snapped out of the frustration and confusion that was rising.

"Let us finish our drinks and we shall go somewhere where it is just the two of us," Avenyx said with a smile.

"I'd like that very much." Ruby agreed, taking a sip of her orange juice and the pair sat and chatted reminiscing on old times for a little.

They laughed and chatted, enjoying another drink until Ruby finally turned the conversation back to what Avenyx wanted to know. "Where would you like me to begin?" she asked. Ruby studied Avenyx's face, she still could not come to terms with how he had not aged a day. She knew this was the way it would always be, but as the years went on for her, it still amazed her more and more.

"Shall we walk? I can concentrate more if we walk and talk," Avenyx said, getting up off his stool.

"As you wish, but not too far-- these old legs are not as young as they used to be."

"Oh of course," Avenyx replied softly, "how thoughtless of me."

"It is fine, a walk in the night air will do me some good." Avenyx smiled, taking hold of Ruby's gloved hand, and escorted her out the doors onto the tavern's steps. He then assisted her down the wooden steps as they walked through the town center.

"Isn't this nice, you and I walking in the light of the moons again?" Avenyx asked, smiling at her.

"Of course, it is," she smiled back," but as always, you avoid asking me the question, which means you know what I have to say will cause you great pain and sorrow."

"I do miss this. I am such a fool for staying away, not only from the town but also from you. Please forgive me."

"You know I always will Avey, however, there is something else on your mind. I think it's time we discuss this to put it at ease. Unlike yourself, time is not on my side, and I will not be buried in a town that has been torn apart by hate. Like you, I have stood aside for too long, not making a stand, but now someone has to, or maybe it is already too late. It's a little funny how it works, your influence, and spell over us all."

Avenyx snickered at this and rolled his eyes at Ruby. She just stared at him for a moment before she continued speaking. "I know you do not like that people look up to and believe in you or the title that you've been given, but you are a God and you always will be. You need to realize everything you do affects the people of this town that still believe in you. With you not being around as much, look what has become of it."

Avenyx came to a halt, and Ruby sternly looked up to him. He was trying to think of a response to this, his brow furrowed causing lines across his forehead.

"I like my whiskey dry Avenyx; you know there is no sugar coating anything with me."

"I always did say that was one of your finer qualities," Avenyx mumbled, but Ruby heard him clear as day.

"The people of this town trusted you, looked up to you, were your friends, but to them, you were so much more; you were their protector, savior. You are their God."

That word again. God. Avenyx hated being called a God. He didn't feel like anything special. In the early days, long before he came to Hazy Foot, he used to enjoy the power and the crowd that looked up to him. That all faded quickly and his sole reason for coming to Hazy Foot was just to be normal and fit in. The town folk of Hazy Foot had offered this. Once they realized he was a God, they did act a little different, but most treated him the same as always after a while, only occasionally asking for special favors, which Avenyx was usually happy to oblige.

"You let them down and abandoned them Avenyx," Ruby continued, pulling Avenyx from his memories. "Where were they meant to turn when the thing they believed in most walked out on them? Do you know what happens to people who lose their faith?" Ruby stopped walking, looking up at Avenyx, waiting for his answer.

"What of the one that governs this town? A town leader is chosen for a reason. Also, as I recall they turned on me. You remember that night just as well as I do. You remember the screams, the yelling, and the hatred. I wish I could have saved them all! Instead, I was sitting at your tavern drinking with my 'friend'. Some protector."

Avenyx was furious and raised his voice a little. Ruby knew he was not angry at her, she knew this was the best way to get through to Avenyx and he knew it also; this was why he had come to her for the answers.

"Funny thing you should ask of the town leader, as I personally believe when the last one was appointed was when things started to change. However, this turn of events was after you walked away, the majority sided with him and well, even though he is no longer around, this is where we are now." Ruby paused for a moment to study Avenyx's puzzled face.

"And where are we now Ruby? Where have they all gone? What happened to them? I've watched this town at night but many homes are now abandoned, this small town now seems tiny with half its residents nowhere to be seen."

"Different reasons. Some left in fear to find a new home, heading for Luccian I believe, it is the next closest town over the swamp and across the fields. Others, sadly like our dear friend Ticcarus, were taken from us before their time." Ruby closed her eyes for a moment and smiled, remembering Ticcarus Valorgrace. "There was also the outbreak of the awful disease, 'Destined to Die'."

Avenyx let out a gasp.

"Yes. I assure you, though, most who obtained it were very careful not to spread such a terrible thing. The disease was marking people for death, turning their blood black. Those who still have it keep to themselves now, but still, it was a hard time. Shall we go back to that night then? In my opinion, it all began there. I believe that would be the best place to start."

Avenyx did not say a word and just listened and nodded at Ruby as they began to walk along the road and speak again.

"All the key players were there that night, and for each of them, something changed. It was such a long time ago but still so fresh in my old mind, as I believe it to be in yours. All this began on the night of the fires."

Puzzled at first, Avenyx began to process what his friend was saying, which triggered a memory he wished he had forgotten, from a dreaded night 10 years ago.

Chapter 4

Ten years earlier, on the night that would be forever referred to as 'The Night of the Fires', there was not an empty seat in sight and people still kept packing in to Ruby's, as it generally was the first night of the three-day break when those who spent the days and nights working came down from the mountains for a little time off. Most came directly to Ruby's as soon as Big Jonas did his final call, signaling it was time for them to pack up and head home to spend with their loved ones. They worked hard on the mountain, breaking stone and rock to build their homes, and in the mines digging out caves and tunnels, hunting for precious gems. Their ox-drawn carts, each filled with at least twenty strong men and women, made the seemingly endless stretch down the mountainside; the same trip week in, week out. The stretch of rocky road continued until it came to another long and dusty road, which was much smoother returning them back to town. On the last day of the working cycle, they finished up early- just after mid-day, as it took until almost nightfall for them to make the trek back. A betting man would gamble his entire wage that by the time both moons rose in the dark night sky, the majority of them would be in Ruby's Tavern with a cold drink in their hand; except for the devoted few that slipped home to see their lovers or families first. Like the sun setting and moons rising, it was expected the workers would go to Ruby's. Whether their journey was in the blistering sun or pouring rain, all the workers on the first night of the break eventually ended up at Ruby's for at least one drink.

As always, Avenyx sat at one of the tables next to the stairs in the darkest corner alone, awaiting his great friend Ticcarus Valorgrace. Such a devoted husband and father would always call in on the way to his loving wife Marni and his two sons, Gaidence and Kendall.

Avenyx chugged down the remainder of a tonic water concoction which was his starter beverage he ordered every time. As he wiped the beads of sweat from his forehead, he noticed a barmaid approaching. She was quite tall, wore black knee-high boots, black stockings, and a knee-length black skirt. Out of the other three barmaids, she was the only one who wore a black blouse, where the other barmaids wore white, with her black apron over top.

"Hot enough night for ya?" she said to Avenyx as she approached, her voice was soft and almost seductive as it came from her full red lips, covered in a deep shade of lipstick. Avenyx looked up into her bright blue eyes as she flicked back her wavy dark brown, almost black hair. Her smile was so warm and genuine when men were finished being distracted by her low-cut blouse they would be drawn in by that smile and those luscious sultry lips.

"A hot night it is indeed," Avenyx agreed.

"Shall I get you a little something to help cool you down?"

"Watch ya' self with that one God, she might try to charm ya back to her house later. Not that I wouldn't say no if she headed on over my way!" A drunk called from a few tables over, licking his lips as he looked the barmaid up and down. Instantly her eyes darted over to the short, rough-looking man who called out the comment. She glared at him, her blue eyes as cold as ice, she could almost pierce his skin with the sharpness of the look she gave. Nervously he turned back to the group he was drinking with.

"Do not listen to their nonsense Jenwa, they are just having a good time and a bit of a laugh after working so hard up in those mountains," Avenyx smiled up to her.

"Can I get you another drink, Avey?" Jenwa asked in a direct tone with the sweetness drained away.

"Indeed you can, and also a whiskey with ice for my friend who has just entered." Jenwa glanced over to the swinging tavern doors and shot a smile across the crowded room to Ticcarus, then headed back behind the bar. Ticcarus was an average height man, but from the years working up the mountain he was well built. With his rugged face and tanned skin, Ticcarus was one of the kindest people in the whole of Hazy Foot. He was dressed neatly in a pair of freshly mended pants and matching brown shirt, his neatly parted short brown hair was freshly washed and shiny. He had cleaned himself up nicely before coming into town for the night, making sure he was well presented. As he pushed his way through the rowdy mob, making his way over to Avenyx's table, many men patted him on the back and welcomed him but he did not stop, he continued to the table he sat at every fourth full moon with his dear friend, the God of Night. Avenyx stood waiting for Ticcarus to sit, then sat again, and they both smiled, happy to see one another.

"Avenyx! By the Gods, it's still warm out there," Ticcarus greeted cheerfully.

"I have just the thing to help with that my friend, already on its way."

"You're a good man Avenyx."

"How are Marni and the boys? I'm sure little Kendall must be starting to be a handful for her."

"Yes, it is coming up to his second double eclipse this year, starting to talk and all now. Marni is coping quite well, and Gaidence helps her out greatly. He wants to work up there with me one day, but Gaidence is a smart boy. I certainly don't want him to waste his life smashing rocks and stones all day. He's a stubborn boy that one."

"He must get that from his father," Avenyx replied with a cheeky grin.

"Maybe I'll just pray to the Gods he doesn't have to, try my luck…" Ticcarus said, with a large smirk on his face.

"Shall I just click my fingers and make it so?" Avenyx smiled back, "If only it was that easy, dear friend."

Jenwa returned with the drinks, placing them on the table.

"Good evening, beautiful lady," Ticcarus said, as he fetched his coin pouch.

"Evening Tic. No need," she said, indicating the pouch, "this one is on the lady at the end of the bar."

Both Avenyx and Ticcarus turned, at the end of the bar in a sparkling red evening gown, with golden curled hair, stood the most elegantly dressed woman in the entire tavern, giggling to one of the young men. Once she realized she now had their attention, she raised her hand to her lips and blew them a kiss. All three laughed and shook their heads.

"Give Ruby our thanks," Avenyx smiled.

"Hey, hussy! We'll have another lot of drinks if ya not too busy working your magic on an old-timer like Tic," a tall, young man called from the table across from them. Jenwa chose to ignore the comment, keeping her smile on her face, hiding what she was truly feeling. However, the smile on Ticcarus' face dropped, and he almost spat out his mouthful of whiskey as he spun around to face the man.

"Young Lirracide Etherthorn, do you wish for me to share the way you speak to women with your mother?" Ticcarus boomed. "And secondly this *old-timer* would have you on the floor crying like a fool in a heartbeat. Similar to the time last wet season, when your girlfriend ran off on you with the pompous gentleman from the next town over." This caused a stir and the men around began to laugh at young Lirracide, causing his face to turn bright red.

"Just repeating what I heard," Lirracide shot back.

"Do not believe everything you hear boy."

"It's fine Tic, I may look like a delicate flower on the outside but it's what inside that counts. These men mean nothing to me, there is nothing they can say which will upset me," Jenwa sighed. "Or haven't you heard? Apparently, I'm a Temptress." Ticcarus and Avenyx watched as Jenwa strutted over to serve the table, leaving the pair looking at one another, extremely unimpressed.

"These young men nowadays Avenyx, I tell you, no manners whatsoever. If I ever treated a lady like that or even spoke those words about a woman, I would have my father's fist to answer to. Please tell me I never acted like that when I was as young as them."

"You, Ticcarus Valorgrace, were nothing but a gentleman to everyone who crossed your path. Holding doors open for people when they would enter, offering to carry heavy baskets of vegetables for struggling women. I tell you, if your boys grow up like you my friend, whoever wins their heart will be very lucky indeed." Avenyx reminded him, taking a sip of his drink.

"I really don't believe she is a Temptress, seducing men and women of the town. Half the young women in this town can't hold a candle to that beauty, besides our dear Ruby, of course. I am a married man, I know, and I love my wife dearly, but sometimes the way that girl looks at me makes me wish I had seen twenty fewer eclipses and was free as a bird."

Avenyx laughed at this, almost spitting out his drink. "Ticcarus you dope, I believe it's all part of a character to make you want to purchase more drinks from our dear friend Ruby. She's a smart woman that Ruby, how else does she manage to run a place like this in our small, hidden away town? Now that you mention it, however, I have noticed the men in here acting a bit different to Jenwa lately, although it's only recently--tonight, and the last break you lot were down. I believed it was just the men having a laugh. After all, it's Jenwa. She's thick-skinned that girl, like she said, she will just shrug it off."

"It's actually a little more than just the names they are calling her. Someone you and I both do not see eye to eye with started this turn of events." Ticcarus took a swig of his whiskey and crunched on a piece of ice, screwing up his face as the mouthful went down.

"Do you care to share this information with me and who this instigator may be?" Avenyx asked, intrigued. Ticcarus was just about to disclose what he had uncovered when Ruby made her way over to the table, pulling up a wooden chair to join the pair.

"Don't mind little old me joining you two handsome young men, do you?" she asked, as she waved a red-feathered fan in front of her face.

"Young men? My dear lady, I believe you are mistaken, I do not see any young men at this table," Avenyx smiled.

"Speak for yourself Avey, there is still youth left in these bones," Ticcarus smirked and the three of them laughed.

The night continued on as Ruby continued to drink with her favorite two customers. Avenyx, having enjoyed the odd whiskey or two, was beginning to feel light-headed. The atmosphere rose, the regular group that often entertained the crowd with their singing and instrument playing had begun, which added to the surrounding noise. The more people drank, the louder and more demanding they became, putting a strain on Ruby's barmaids. Now and then she would call out to them, pointing out if they had missed a table or if they needed to clean up a spill. Ruby was a hard woman to work for, although she paid extremely well and always backed her girls when the clients of the tavern got a little out of hand. On a few occasions, she had thrown people out and told them to go home and sleep it off, as they were having a bit too much fun, drinking a little too much, or getting a little too mouthy with her girls. Never would anyone disagree or argue with Ruby, she was the most respected woman in all of Hazy Foot.

The tavern had been in Ruby's bloodline as far back as She could remember. Ruby was the name of her grandmother, and believed to be the name of her grandmother's grandmother. Many, many double eclipses ago, when Avenyx first came to Hazy Foot, a Ruby had been the owner at that time. Avenyx had always been close to Ruby's family, and Avenyx was worried as Ruby never married and did not have children of her own. She was the last in the line and had no one to hand down the tavern to when it was her time to leave the world of Thera. Avenyx had tried to bring this up with her on a few occasions, but every time he tried, Ruby would put on a sultry voice and ask if Avenyx was insinuating something. Even though Ruby would never reveal her age, everyone knew she was getting on in her years. In her younger years and possibly still now to some degree, she could have the pick of any man she wanted in the town. She was graceful, elegant, womanly, and extremely wealthy. Ruby never felt that special something with any of the men of Hazy Foot, she generally didn't give most men the time of day when it came to romance. Ruby always aimed high, she had her eyes on someone though over the years, someone who made her heart flutter. The only one who had caught Ruby's fancy was not a man but a God. But Ruby being Ruby was the type of woman who generally got what she wanted and if she could not, she would not settle for anything else and went without.

"You mean to say, you believe this all began that night so long ago?" Avenyx asked.

"I'm just trying to put it all in perspective for you Avey."

"I remember the details thank you, Ruby. But what did happen to the town? Tell me why the baker no longer opens? Why are the lanterns at night no longer lit? Where are the children that used to play in the street? And why have so many moved on?"

"They're afraid, I guess. With no one to protect or watch over them…" Ruby paused allowing this to sink in a little, before linking her arm with Avenyx's.

"Come now," she said, "let us walk a little more, it's such a nice night for it."

Chapter 5

"Do you remember Avey? On every fourth day when the blue moon was full, Elenora Willamyst would traipse through the main street of town sharing her wisdom of the Gods. Trying to trade her knock-off 'By the Gods' blessed beads of holiness," Ruby asked Avenyx grinning.

"You were always so harsh to that dear woman," Avenyx shook his head but Ruby could sense a smile was lurking in the darkness on his face.

"Are you going to stand here and tell me she was the genuine thing, sent here by the Gods to share their message?"

"Well of course not my dear, we 'Gods'," every time he said the word Ruby could sense him cringe or racking his brain to find better wording but knowing this was the only word for his kind, "wouldn't use a messenger. We are just here to lend a helping hand. You, my friend, know me well enough to know I care not whether Elenora, or you for that matter, believe in me, follow me, or even worship me."

"Avenyx. The God of Denial."

Avenyx stopped walking again and Ruby paused beside him, he looked down into her sparkling eyes and wondered, as he often used to, how such a graceful woman could ever be so harsh and to the point.

"She did, you know?" Avenyx twitched his head to the side not recalling what Ruby was referring to. "I remember when she met you and claimed you were a fraud or imposter, in her dying days, she prayed and called out to you many a time. When you did not come, she knew it was because it was her time. She also knew that you would protect her son, and help him once again as you had in the past. As her son was special or tainted, depends on who you ask and what their perspective on the world is. Although in her words her son had been given a gift from the Gods themselves."

"Who is this boy you speak of? I do not recall." Avenyx was intrigued. Over his time in Hazy Foot, many of the children were born with abilities and gifts. Most developed them further as they grew older and even some that were not born with these, studied and sorted out magical ways on their own. The fascination and enthusiasm for it slowly evened out over time, still few would often seek out Avenyx for advice, answers, and knowledge, when they did, he would help them as best he could. Avenyx acquired so much knowledge over time, and was always more than happy to assist. Whether it be an understanding ear that would listen, providing books filled with knowledge, or offering tips on how to control their special abilities. And what he didn't know or have access to, he would point them in the right direction to find. Even on a couple of occasions, he advised where they might be able to find another God or Goddess with a better understanding of the gift the individual possessed. Although Avenyx rarely kept in contact with the other Gods and Goddesses, there was something inside that drew them all together as one. A little feeling or more like a sense. All he had to do is close his eyes and picture them and he could tell the location of where they were in Thera. Sometimes he could feel their pain or sadness, where other times he could feel great amounts of happiness or pleasure. Generally, these were feelings Avenyx chose to ignore as he felt his time with the others had passed long ago.

"You do not remember him, do you?" Ruby asked and Avenyx shook his head.

"You do not remember Aquillarus Willamyst, the young boy who wanted to be an Elementalist?" As the name came from Ruby's dry lips, Avenyx's skin crawled and was shivering all over before she could complete her sentence. Avenyx knew this boy's name very well although he did not piece together the connection to his mother at first.

"Young Aquillarus was there that night also."

"I do believe you are a little bit tipsy my friend," Ticcarus laughed as he chugged down half a glass of whiskey.

"Ticcarus Valorgrace, I strongly disagree with you and find that you, my friend, are mistaken," Avenyx replied, pointing at Ticcarus, although by the time he had finished the sentence he had swayed a little and his hand was now pointing at Ruby who sat next to him. Ruby laughed, taking hold of Avenyx's hand and slowly moving it back so he was pointing at Ticcarus. Avenyx smiled at Ruby as he felt her soft hands touching his. He loved her touch, so gentle, her skin was so soft; he often sat thinking to himself, how much he just wanted to feel her hands on his face. This secret thought was something he could not share with anyone, as he knew, in the end, it would only lead to heartbreak and as he was a God, he could never fully give himself to anyone. It would cause much more pain than it was worth. Avenyx pulled his hand away from Ruby's and lifted his glass to finish the remaining whiskey, smiling across the table at Ticcarus.

Over at the far end of the bar, a younger man with scruffy auburn hair, barely old enough to be drinking at the tavern, was amusing a crowd of drunken onlookers.

"Show me again boy," an elderly man slurred almost falling off his barstool.

"Buy me one of Ruby's finest brews and I will be happy to," the young man smiled with a cheeky grin on his face.

"You heard him lass, a glass of Ruby's finest brew for the boy," he instructed Jenwa. She poured the young man a drink and took the copper coins from the drunken man.

Jenwa leaned over as she handed the scruffy-haired boy his drink and whispered in his ear, "you best be careful with your little conjuring tricks, young Aquillarus, wouldn't want the wrong person seeing and you getting a name for yourself."

"Thanks for the warning, love, but I can take care of myself," Aquillarus grinned back.

"Don't say I didn't warn you," Jenwa said and walked away to serve another patron.

"Watch closely now," he told the elderly man as he took a large gulp of brew, then picked up a glass half-filled with water. He placed it on the bar in front of him and rolled up the sleeves of his black shirt, he then began to stare at the water with full concentration. He raised his hands and began to stretch out his fingers, then slowly bringing them back in towards his palms.

He was now doing this rhythmically, not breaking concentration. The water ever so slowly began to swirl until it rose in the glass.

The old man gasped, which gained the attention of others who were closest to him. They joined in to watch in amazement.

Aquillarus continued the motion with his fingers then slowly closed his eyes. The water rose higher until it was completely out of the glass. Still swirling, it began to form a ball of water in the air. As if on its own it continued, the ball of water expanded until the half glass of water would easily be able to fill at least four glasses of the same size.

Aquillarus opened his eyes still grinning at the old man; he stopped moving his fingers keeping his hands up and wide open. Slowly he moved his hands towards one another and the ball of water stopped swirling and began to shrink. During the process Aquillarus felt a shove in his back, he lost his concentration and spun around to face whoever had bumped into him. As Aquillarus turned, the ball of water followed until it splashed into the man standing behind him, saturating his face.

Aquillarus dropped his hands immediately and pulled a blue handkerchief from his shirt pocket, handing it to the man.

"I'm awfully sorry, sir," Aquillarus apologized, in his squeaky breaking voice as the man snatched the handkerchief and began to wipe his face. The man handed it back, Aquillarus looked into the dark brown eyes glaring at him, filled with hatred. The man was a lot taller than Aquillarus and much beefier than Aquillarus' scrawny build. His face was rough and his dark brown hair, which was now wet, was roughly parted to the left.

"You will be sorry, boy!" he sternly replied with his voice raised.

"It's just a little something I was showing my friend here."

"It should be forbidden. Using abilities, showing off to get free drinks. Are you even old enough to be in this place?" he asked Aquillarus as he shoved him against the bar.

"I'll have you know, I've seen my sixteenth double eclipse, making me of age to work in the mountains with everyone else, therefore I can drink in this fine establishment with those that work just as hard as I." Aquillarus puffed his chest out to confront the man.

"Come now, you do not want trouble, or for me to get Ruby involved," Jenwa said, making her way over, placing herself between the two men trying to stop the confrontation, not fully aware of the situation. She did not realize at first who Aquillarus was having this quarrel with until she was face to face with the man.

"Did I not warn you to stay away from me? I am no longer under your spell harlot!" the man said, loud enough to draw even more attention and for half of the tavern to fall silent and listening to the brewing commotion.

"Listen here, your lies have done enough damage to me. How about we leave it be, we both know the truth," Jenwa replied, almost whispering, gritting her teeth.

"You threaten to tell my wife, I got there first. One thing you should have learned about me, my dear. I always win," he said quietly back to her. Aquillarus wanted to aid Jenwa and stand up for her but he knew not to get involved. "I suggest you move out the way and let the men sort this one out. I know you are used to controlling men but get behind the bar where you belong." The man spoke loudly again to the audience he'd attracted. This upset Jenwa quite a bit, but she knew how much she needed this work. She promised Ruby she would keep her cool and not let her anger get in the way. She stared the man down for a moment, then walked away but as she did, she called out nice and loud.

"Ruby! You need to deal with our friend Millerson Thact!"

Avenyx continued to slowly walk with Ruby at his side until she came to a stop and raised her hand to her mouth in an attempt to cover a yawn, however it was not as effective as she hoped.

"A little tired?" Avenyx asked.

"Not as young as I used to be, cannot be wandering the streets until the sun comes up with tall, handsome strangers like I used to."

"Then I shall escort you home."

"Only if you promise to come see me again soon and not keep a girl waiting as long this time. It's been too long, Avey, and since you have decided to show your face around again, I would like to see it a lot more."

"You have my word." Avenyx gave her a little tilt of his head as he said this.

As promised, he escorted Ruby back to her tavern then whisked away into the night.

Gaidence stood impatiently outside of the old beaten down chicken coop. He was waiting for his brother in the same spot he had met him the night before. He looked around constantly in the darkness in hope that his brother would be there soon. He searched nearby bushes. He climbed to the top of the coop, constantly whispering his brother's name into the night. Gaidence realized his brother wasn't going to show up, which led him to become more concerned than usual.

Although he spent time with his brother earlier during the day, Kendall did seem slightly distracted; more distracted than usual. he was also in a hurry to leave before night fell and when Gaidence asked him to meet him again, although Kendall nodded his reply, Gaidence felt it was half-hearted.

For a while now Kendall had been staying away at night, he told Gaidence he had a vision, when "they" come for him, it will be at night. Although Kendall did not know who "they" were, he said he knew their faces from around the town, and "they" will eventually capture him since he is tainted. Gaidence constantly fought with his younger brother, telling him he would be safe and he would protect him, but Kendall assured Gaidence some things are just set in stone and that they happened for a reason. This was one of those things. Gaidence struggled with this concept and could not understand it completely. He believed if he stood in the way of this event, preventing it from happening, the outcome would change. This had always been Gaidence's way of thinking; he loved to question or challenge things. Even when he was growing up and his mother taught him of the Gods, he questioned them. When his mother told him to eat all his dinner so he would grow up to be strong, he questioned her. When his father warned him not to play in the rain, as he would become ill, Gaidence challenged him just to prove him wrong. A failed attempt, however, as

Gaidence spent the next two full moons in bed, recovering from the worst fever he had ever experienced. So when his little brother told him of a vision that revealed he would be taken by the uprising crusade, due to his gift, Gaidence said he would do what he could to challenge this.

"Waiting for someone Gade?" A voice startled him. He froze, a little afraid to turn around but he did so, slowly turning to face who was standing behind him.

A young man around the same age as Gaidence, stood before him. Someone who was once his friend, and Gaidence was once an only friend for him. But now how things had changed. Jacobus was always the odd one out in a group. He was always a little chubbier, mouthier, complained a lot, and generally rubbed most people the wrong way. He would always try to gain peopled attention and wanted to be accepted, sadly most would try not to involve him and leave him out. Gaidence, feeling sorry for the boy, chose to be friends with him when others would not. For a long while now, so many of Gaidence's friends have moved away with their families or just drifted apart, resulting in Gaidence generally being on his own. His friendship with Jacobus drifted apart when Jacobus' opinions on things started to change. Jacobus would always have a way to find faults in others, bully those for looking different and just developed a negative outlook on the world. Not wanting part of this, Gaidence slowly saw him less.

This, along with the fact that Gaidence had other matters of importance going on. Some of this time was spent looking after his mother, who did not take his father's death too well. He cared for her all the way up until the time she left. She disappeared late one night, leaving a note saying she is going in search of a God who will be able to bring back their father. Which then left Gaidence to take care of just his brother. He had to grow up rather quickly and learned about other priorities, such as keeping up with the chores at home, coming to town to trade and get supplies, doing odd jobs for the people of the town to earn what little copper he could to keep the two of them going.

"Just out for a nightly stroll, I like it at night; it's nice and quiet," Gaidence replied, and prepared himself to walk away. He knew Jacobus was alone but sensed he still wanted to start some trouble. Gaidence thought he could probably take him on, but knew it would be best just to run. Jacobus must have sensed this was Gaidence's plan and stood directly in front of him so he could not make his escape.

"No little friend dressed in all black tonight to come to your rescue? You know, I still haven't gotten you back for your little darkness trick in the alley last night. Turns out you are just as tainted as your little brother." Gaidence's eyes narrowed and he clenched his fist at his side.

"That was not me, Jacobus. Be warned though, I do not need a God at my side to win a battle with you."

"A God you say? So the stories are true and the God has returned. Well, the tainted do need a leader. I mean someone has to control the bunch of mismatched freaks that just don't fit in. After what we are planning and with our numbers growing every time the sun rises…"

"You do not understand what you are saying. You want to join something you are not fully aware of. The Gods would not take sides."

"Do you speak for them now, Gade? Gade the Godspeaker! What would you know anyway? And yes the Gods would take sides! They already do. These Gods are just as wicked as these *gifted*. You see, the tainted is just the starting mark for a great plan of purification. May we go after that God friend of yours. A God— that is a nice goal to work towards and what the heck, why stop at just the one, there are plenty of them out there. Or so they say. We could eventually wipe them all out."

"The Gods do not want some great battle! You think they really care about some ludicrous mission of hate you have joined. They are here to protect and watch over all of us, not just those who are gifted."

"You see this is where you are wrong, my friend."

"This is where YOU are mistaken, Jacobus. I am no longer a friend of yours. Not since you began to hunt my brother at night like he is prey. A boy who is five years younger than you are. Such an easy target, but still you insist on hunting him. And why? To prove you are worthy to your new friends and to someone who I pity more than I do yourself. You target this boy because he is gifted."

In a fit of frustration, Jacobus gave Gaidence a mighty shove, knocking him to the ground, shouting, "TAINTED!"

Gaidence hated the word, he hated his brother being called this, being labeled in such a way. He hated it so much that people had started categorizing him, treating his brother differently from and ignoring him completely. Because of whispers and rumors around town. Whispers and rumors which none can prove are true.

Gaidence wanted to put a stop to it all. He quickly rose to his feet and with a quick right hook, Gaidence's fist smashed into Jacobus' face. Jacobus's head snapped back then he retaliated by raising his fists, taking a swing back. But Gaidence was prepared this time and bounced backward, avoiding Jacobus' strike. Jacobus took another swing, this time, as he did Gaidence grabbed hold of his fist, stopping it from making contact. Gaidence firmed his grip on Jacobus's hand.

"You're wasting my time, leave me be," Gaidence warned.

Jacobus broke Gaidence's hold and retracted his arm, he raised his short leg, kicking it towards Gaidence who raised his leg to block the kick but was struck in the shin.

Gaidence let out a groan of pain and stopped holding back. He charged forward in rage, knocking Jacobus to the ground, and sat on top of him, pinning him there. He shoved his shoulder furiously as Jacobus made an attempt to get up, "You are a fool, Jacobus. A FOOL! We are all equal. No sides! No normal or gifted! Your hair is black and mine is brown, but I'm not going to go off and join a brown hair crusade. Everyone is different but we should still treat one another as equal."

Gaidence slammed his shoulders against the hard earth. He peered down into Jacobus's large brown eyes that just stared back up at him. Gaidence could see a small trickle of blood on the corner of his mouth where he'd punched him.

"I bet your brother didn't see this coming," Jacobus smiled, then spat in Gaidence's face. Gaidence jumped up immediately, disgusted, and began wiping his face. Jacobus took his opportunity, kicking Gaidence in the shin again causing him to keel over in pain. He then kicked him again in the stomach, winding Gaidence. Gaidence was on his hands and knees trying to catch his breath. Jacobus kicked him one last time with the final blow landing in Gaidence's side, and he collapsed in a heap, curling in on himself and moaning in pain.

"We will get your brother. And we will get the God. This is just the beginning Gade, you should join us now while you can. Who knows? We might decide to come after you, just for siding with the Tainted." Jacobus spat on Gaidence again before running off, leaving him on the ground. Gaidence laid in pain for a moment then tears began to stream down his face.

"He's not Tainted! My brother is just a boy. HE'S NOT TAINTED!" he shouted out into the dark night. Exhausted, bruised and beaten Gaidence couldn't do much more. His body ached and his mind raced. Determined not to give in, but he no longer had a choice as he collapsed to the ground as unconsciousness eventually overtook him.

Chapter 6

Ruby stood radiantly in the morning sun on the wooden porch of her tavern. She wore a long, deep red skirt that went all the way down to her ankles with a white and red floral blouse, along with a red rose in her hair which she wore in a side bun opposite to the rose. She was ordering her worker Leeif around, with the wave of her hands.

"No, I want flower boxes, young man. At either end and two at the front. I want the beautiful aroma of flowers wafting as you enter the doors, out of the heat of the warm sun," Ruby explained.

"You're in an awfully cheerful mood today, if I may say so Miss Ruby," Leeif politely smiled up to her.

Leeif was in his early twenties and had worked for Ruby for the last few years. Due to an accident when he was much younger, Leeif had deep scars all over his body, including his face. No one quite knew what happened to him, however, the scars came in a variety of shapes and sizes. Some looked like they may have been cuts, while others appeared as burns or lesions. Leeif began working up in the mountains as the majority of the young men of Hazy Foot do after their sixteenth double eclipse. But it's tough up there and if you don't fit in, you get forced out pretty quickly. They used to make fun of Leeif's disfigurements, calling him weak and making him feel very uncomfortable. One night Leeif came to the Tavern, after quite a few whiskeys, he poured his heart out to Ruby, he explained how he didn't like being treated differently because of the way he looked. He said the mountains were a terrible place to work but it got him away from home, yet he felt trapped trying to constantly pick between the lesser of two evils. Ruby felt sorry for the boy, offering him to come work for her. This arrangement also included a new home at the Tavern when Leeif was thrown out by his father for, as he put it, 'not being a real man' and working up at the mountains. So Leeif took up occupancy in one of the upstairs rooms in Ruby's Tavern. His mother and father soon after moved away and Leeif had not heard from them since. Ruby always had the slight suspicion that someone in the family was gifted or had a secret to hide, however, she was not one to pry. Ruby accepted people for who or what they were, she was never one to question Leeif, she made him aware if he needed to talk about anything, she was always there for him.

"Young Leeif, you may be correct in your observation, however, chatting about my mood will not get the job done. I suggest you go round the back, grab a few planks of wood, a hammer, some strong nails, and get to work on making me those flower boxes," Ruby ordered.

Leeif just giggled to himself, Ruby was a hard woman and made him earn his keep, but he wouldn't have it any other way.

Before Leeif had a chance to rush off to action Ruby's request, something caught his eye--someone was staggering down the dirt road into town. They were hunched over, clutching onto their side, as they slowly staggered closer towards the Tavern dragging their feet.

"Miss Ruby…" Leeif began to alert the tavern owner, but she had already noticed, hitching up her skirt and making her way down the creaky wooden steps and out onto the street toward the injured party. Leeif quickly followed behind.

Like most days, the town center was deserted, although Milliantil's vegetable and fruits store were open, she was almost always out the back as people rarely visited. It was still quite early in the morning for anyone else to be in town, so Ruby and Leeif were the only ones who rushed to a bruised and beaten Gaidence's aid. As they got closer, he called out to them in a very hoarse voice, "Have you seen Kendall? I can't find him anywhere."

As Ruby and Leeif reached him, he collapsed at their feet. Ruby instantly bent down placing her hand on his forehead then touching his dry parched lips.

"Leeif, quickly head back to the Tavern. Fetch me a bucket of cold water and a towel, the boy is burning up," Ruby ordered and he rushed off obediently. Ruby turned her attention back to the boy. "Gaidence! Gaidence Valorgrace!" Ruby called his name but he did not open his eyes. Shaking him ever so slightly, Ruby was still unable to wake him. She studied the patches of dry blood on his face and hands. Ruby slowly lifted his dirty and torn beige button-up shirt to inspect the side he clung to as he approached. She'd imagined how clean it would have been when he had put it on. The Valorgrace's were always clean boys, their clothes were always neat and respectable, Ruby knew this was a trait they picked up from their father.

As Ruby peered at his side, hidden behind the shirt was a large bruised area. His once soft pink skin was now a dark shade of purple, almost black. The bruising spread from his side, as it curved around, touching both his back and also came around the front covering a small portion of his chest. Ruby pulled his shirt back down covering the injury and shook her head, "Who has done such a thing to you my boy?" she whispered. By this time Leeif had returned with the metal bucket, half-filled with water and a not so clean white towel, he'd used recently for cleaning the bar. Ruby looked up at Leeif, taking the towel shaking her head, "You didn't think to get a clean one?"

"Sorry ma'am, I was trying to hurry," he replied, placing the bucket next to her.

"Understood," she nodded, as she placed the towel in the bucket saturating it with water.

"Take his shirt off for me," Ruby ordered.

Without questioning, Leeif went down and began to unbutton Gaidence's shirt. Gaidence let out a quiet groan but stayed unconscious.

"Be careful! He's injured."Ruby began to wring out the towel, then dabbed Gaidence's lips and wiped down his forehead. Leeif winced as he noticed the bruising. Ever so slowly, he tried to get Gaidence's arm out of the sleeve.

Noticing Leeif was struggling, Ruby returned the towel to the bucket of water and assisted. Once they had successfully removed his shirt, Ruby began to use the wet towel to clean the wounded area with care. Gaidence began to stir a little and as he slowly came around, he pushed Ruby away, calling out Kendall's name.

Leeif helped Ruby to her feet. Gaidence, realizing what he had just done began to apologize, "Miss Ruby my sincerest apology, I did not mean you any harm." He attempted to stand but he was in too much pain.

"It's fine, do not try to move young Gaidence Valorgrace, your injuries are too great and I am guessing in the morning heat you are extremely parched." Gaidence just nodded.

"What has happened to you?" Ruby asked. Gaidence just tried to turn his head as if he was searching for someone.

"I woke up in the fields, I must have passed out there. I really must find my brother ma'am," Gaidence whispered, as if he was losing his voice and he either couldn't speak or it pained him too much too.

"We must get you inside. If we lift you to your feet, with our aid, can you make it to the Tavern?" Ruby asked, and Gaidence nodded. Ruby pointed to the bucket and Gaidence's shirt on the ground, Leeif put the shirt into the bucket, picked it up, and with his free hand he helped Gaidence to his feet. As he did, Gaidence let out a loud groan, then placed an arm around Leeif's shoulder, linked the other with Ruby's arm, and they slowly walked Gaidence to the Tavern.

Once inside, Leeif and Ruby helped Gaidence up onto the bar and laid him on it.

"I'll be fine, honestly. I really need to--" Gaidence protested trying to sit back up.

"You will lay there, even if I have to tie you down. I am taking care of your injuries, and then making you rest. When I say you can go out searching for your brother, you may leave. If you do not wish to share how you got this way, so be it, but that is how things are going to happen." Ruby demanded.

"I've learned it's best you do as she says, she will get her own way in the end anyway," Leeif shrugged.

"Fine!" Gaidence groaned, slamming himself back on the bar, then realized this was a bad move and hissed through his teeth trying to hold back the pain.

"Leeif we need a glass of water, a *clean* bucket of water with a *clean* towel, some bandages, a bottle of whiskey, and a glass with ice in it… make it two glasses with ice."

"Right away!" Leeif replied, leaping over the bar rushing around, gathering items he was ordered to retrieve.

"Are you injured anywhere else? Where else are you in pain?" Ruby asked Gaidence as she pulled up a stall at the bar.

"My leg, and the pain is all over," he replied in a dry tone, flicking his eyes at Ruby then back to the ceiling.

"You'll need to be more specific than that I'm afraid, or shall I just start prodding areas waiting for you to scream?"

Gaidence sighed knowing Ruby was only trying to help him but he could not stop worrying about Kendall. He knew though, he would not be going anywhere soon, or at least until she was convinced he was recovered.

"My left leg, on the front around my shin, he gave me a mighty kick there. The main source of pain is coming from my side and my ribs ma'am."

With this knowledge, Ruby rolled up the left leg of Gaidence's black trousers to reveal another bruise across his shin; it was not as severe, but there was a small cut that ran up his calf also.

Leeif returned with bandages under his arm, a metal bucket of water dangling from the other with a clean towel draped over it, a half bottle of whiskey in one hand and in the other, he was holding with his fingers two small glasses half-filled with ice. Ruby looked up at the young man struggling as he began to put everything down on the bar behind Gaidence's head.

"Where is the glass of water?" she asked.

"Coming ma'am," Leeif replied, continued unloading, and went off again.

Ruby picked up the whiskey, removed the cork stopper, and poured a decent amount into each of the glasses. She picked up a glass and handed it to Gaidence.

"What is this for?" He asked, taking the glass unsure.

"Trust me, take a swig, you'll need it," Ruby replied, taking the other glass, swishing back the contents, leaving the ice still in the glass, all without so much as batting an eyelid. She placed the glass back on the bar, filling it with whiskey again.

"I'm not really a drinker, thank you all the same," Gaidence explained, beginning to put the glass down.

"Drink up," Ruby ordered back. Gaidence raised his head from the bar and took a sip of the whiskey. His eyes widened quickly then he coughed a little and placed the glass down next to him.

"It's a bit rough, but you get used to it."

Gaidence continued to cough a little, then once he stopped he laid his head back down, glancing at the candelabra hanging from the ceiling. Ruby picked up the towel and poured some whiskey on the corner of it then began to dab it onto the cut on Gaidence's leg. Instantly Gaidence bolted upright.

"For the love of the Gods!" he screamed out in pain. Leeif returned at this point and set down the glass of water.

"Did you forget to warn him it was going to hurt a little ma'am?" he asked, with a grin across his face. He took Gaidence by the shoulders and slowly eased him back to lay on the bar, but kept his hands on his shoulders to prevent him from sitting up again. "She gets forgetful in her old age," Leeif whispered in Gaidence's ear.

"It's either that or have your leg fall off," Ruby said, attending to the wound again. Gaidence hissed through his teeth, clenched his fists, and dug his fingernails into the palms of his hands. Once she had finished attending the cuts, she used the other end of the towel, placing it in the water to clean the bruised area, then proceeded to remove the dirt from Gaidence's face and hands. Leeif let go of Gaidence's shoulders and watched Ruby do her work. Her kind, and caring hands, slowly wiping away the dirt. Leeif admired how Ruby was so rough yet so delicate at the same time. Once she was finished, she drank her whiskey and encouraged Gaidence to drink his and he did.

"The water was for you Leeif," Ruby smiled.

"Why thank you, ma'am," Leeif replied gratefully, and drank the water.

After drinking the glass of whisky, Gaidence went to lie back down but Ruby's old hand stopped him.

"I'll need you to sit for this part boy. Leeif, give me a hand to wrap the bandages around his chest." Together, Ruby and Leeif wrapped Gaidence's wounds until his injured chest and leg were covered, then finally Gaidence lay back on the bar.

"It may be a little difficult to get you up the stairs to rest at this stage, so I recommend you just lay here and close your eyes a bit. We don't usually get any patrons stopping by this early in the day but if we do, Leeif and I will be around," Ruby suggested. Gaidence did not disobey and closed his eyes.

"Thank you," he whispered as he slowly drifted off to sleep.

"May the Gods protect you," Ruby replied, got up from her stool and kissed Gaidence on the forehead, then helped Leeif clear away the items from the bar.

Chapter 7

Millerson Thact kept his head down, as he slowly made his way along the dirt road heading directly to Ruby's. He was unsure how his reappearance would be perceived, especially now, yet at the same time, he didn't really care. He had business to attend to and he wanted to get it over with quickly. He was once a popular man and Governor of the town, but his popularity has long since passed. This was largely due to his mysterious departure from the town one night, just over four years ago.

At first, people would query how such a man like Millerson Thact would just up and leave, but as time went on their interest waned, untill Millerson Thact was just a memory to most and this is how Ruby preferred it to be. He was extremely arrogant and self-loving but still many of the men looked up to and admired him. There were rumors that some had seen Millerson camped a day or two outside of town and there were whispers of him making a return. Most of them talking about him were young and impressionable, they probably did not know better but Millerson could turn people over to his way of thinking. It wasn't a gift as such, it's just he knew the right words to say to get people to believe his side of things. This was something he could do since he was a little boy. Millerson came to Hazy Foot just after he had seen his tenth double eclipse with his mother, no one knew where or what happened to Millerson's father but no one really cared to ask. One thing that attracted most to Hazy Foot was that people never used to care much about other people's business. Although everyone basically knew one another, they did not know details and that's how they liked it. Nobody needed to know that Bristora the pig farmer's daughter was really Terrinik's child, that he had an ongoing affair with Bristora's wife for many years. Or that Sylinaria would spend all the copper her partner made up in the mountains on special moonshine from Ruby's, hiding it in the grain jar to sneak swigs of it regularly. These are the types of things that the people kept to themselves, so when a young woman moved to the town with just her son, no one asked questions they just welcomed them. Although as Millerson grew older he did not like the fact no one asked about his past so he used to make up stories. Great stories, such as his father drowning in the sea or eaten alive by a creature from the great Jungle. Millerson loved to tell a story and what he loved more was people believing a story he told, but there was one who did not; his name was Ticcarus Valorgrace.

At the night of Millerson's and Ticcarus' sixteenth double eclipse, Millerson thought he'd tell Ticcarus's newly found lady friend Marni, that Ticcarus was trying to get her intoxicated to have his way with her. He then continued to advise Marni what she needed was a real man to take care of her. Marni did not believe this until Ticcarus came walking out of Ruby's holding two glasses of sparkling cider. Upon presenting Marni with a glass, she took it then poured it to the ground at Ticcarus' feet, storming off, leaving Ticcarus alone with Millerson. After confronting Millerson on what he said, Millerson eventually told Ticcarus. Ticcarus, although very frustrated, did not strike him and only said one thing, "may the Gods forgive you Millerson Thact." Then stormed off leaving Millerson puzzled.

The Gods he thought… Millerson had only heard very little of these Gods before, let alone met someone who actually believed they really existed. He was extremely perplexed that Ticcarus Valorgrace really thought that he would need the God's forgiveness for such a harmless bit of fun. He then pondered the statement again *May the Gods forgive you.* were they watching now, shaking their almighty heads at him? What did these Gods truly think of him, and did they really care too much for this action, or did they have better things to do with their time. This is something

Millerson thought about for many years to come. What made people believe in the Gods or anything really, more importantly, the power they had. The power to gain people's trust so much so that they will believe whatever you say. How he wanted to be that person, and lucky for him in time he was.

Millerson stood at the edge of the town center facing the double story tavern at the end of the road before him. His eyes glaring in disgust, thinking of how much he hated that tavern. He shook his head then spat on the ground as he remembered back to the dreadful night, ten eclipses ago, the last time he stood in Ruby's Tavern.

"Millerson Thact and Aquillarus Willamyst! Causing a disturbance in my Tavern," Ruby called, as she rose from her seat, the crowd of people parted to make a path for her to walk through towards the bar. The tavern was now almost silent with everyone watching every move Ruby made, except those still chatting in the back corner, too intoxicated to realize something else was taking place. Everyone knew when Ruby raised her voice, you better listen and there were only a very few that challenged her. Millerson Thact was one of them.

"Always you, isn't it Millerson? Where there is trouble, your name is attached to it. If there is a bar fight, you're right there on the sidelines. One of my girls was almost in tears and I see them walking away from you. A broken chair and the pieces are lying at your feet."

"What can I say, I'm a popular guy, and sometimes this attracts the wrong crowd," Millerson replied smugly.

"Are you causing trouble with this boy ?" Ruby asked.

"This *boy* was using his undesirable taint, and he covered me in water."

"Undesirable taint? How many whiskeys have you had Millerson?" Ruby asked, not following.

"His corruption!" Millerson said harshly, raising his voice now getting angry.

"I think he means my elemental abilities mam. Avenyx has been helping me develop them I was experimenting with the water and Mister Thact accidentally bumped into me, that's when it spilled on him. It was my mistake honestly ma'ma, I am extremely sorry. I'm willing to buy him a drink to make up for it," Aquillarus apologized nervously to Ruby, brushing his fringe of fiery auburn hair from his face then returning his glance to the ground, while he fished around in his pants pockets for some change to purchase a drink.

"Your apology is accepted. Buying Mister Thact a drink is certainly not necessary and I commend you practicing your gift," Ruby paused then stared into Millerson's dark eyes, "Although my Tavern is a welcoming place, I… we accept all kinds here." She now turned her glance back to Aquillarus, "be careful where you practice your gift and who is around you when doing so." She placed one hand gently on Aquillarus' shoulder with the other placed it under his chin, lifting his head so he was looking up at her.

"Mister Willamyst, always look into a lady's eyes when she is addressing you." Ruby looked deeply into his green eyes, Aquillarus looked back too afraid to turn away, hoping Ruby would break the stare first. He knew he was the youngest in the tavern and did not wish to upset her. He had heard so many stories from the others of her throwing them out, evening tossing them through the windows, and smashing bottles over their heads to break up fights. Although he had never seen this happen in the short time he had been coming to Ruby's, he was certain the woman who had seen almost fifty double eclipses had it in her.

"Now young Elementalist, I will say good night to you. You will head home and I will see you again next time you visit." Ruby gave him a grin, turned on her heel, and walked off. Aquillarus knew he had got off lightly, so he chugged down the remainder of his drink then went to leave, as he did Millerson's hand stopped him by grabbing him fiercely on his shoulder.

"This is not over tainted misfit, people like you don't belong," Millerson said, and Aquillarus broke free of Millerson's grip and rushed out the Tavern.

"Trouble with Millerson Thact again?" Avenyx asked, as Ruby returned to her seat.

"When is there not trouble with Millerson Thact?" Ticcarus asked.

"Yes, we all know where you stand with him, thank you Ticcarus," Ruby said, waving her hand in the air to holler over a barmaid. Ticcarus looked across the table to Avenyx for support.

"I'm not getting involved my friend, you know I support you all the way, nor do I care what the man thinks of me?" Avenyx said, finishing his drink.

"*Gods, pfft. What have they ever done for me? They let my mother die. All they are is a group of high and mighty people that we are stuck with forever. Strutting around thinking they are better than the rest of us. Listen to me and listen well, their days are numbered. The Gods' days will come to an end and when they do, I hope I'm there to watch it.*" Ticcarus recited, doing his best impression of Millerson Thact.

"Is this an 'I hate Millerson Thact meeting'? If so, I want in," Jenwa said, as she approached the table.

"Sadly for you my dear you're not here to be a part of any meeting. Have you not forgotten I'm paying you to serve drinks and that is what you are going to do? We will have another round thank you," Ruby ordered.

"Of course mam," Jenwa replied giving a fake grin.

"I'm glad to see you have worked on your tricks of deception, I am almost convinced you are having a good night," Avenyx said, giving Jenwa a slight wink.

"Just one of my many tricks, just ask Millerson. I'm sure he will have plenty more to tell you about. Seems he's told almost everyone else. Oh, wait a moment, he doesn't like you either so I can only imagine what he says about you," Jenwa said, holding her smile and returned to the bar.

"Avenyx, she is a very beautiful *young* woman and if you wish to fraternize with her please do, but not do it on my time." Ruby glared at Avenyx then got out of her chair.

"I believe you were just told off my friend," Ticcarus laughed.

"Ticcarus Valorgrace. We are dancing!" Ruby said, as she walked away from the table.

Avenyx laughed as Ticcarus followed Ruby away from the table.

Avenyx sat alone for a moment, finished his drink while staring through the crowd at Millerson. He could make out the evil grin across his proud face as he laughed with his friend over the recent incident that just took place. He knew he would be extremely impressed with himself, getting Aquillarus thrown out the way he did. Avenyx had enjoyed getting to know Aquillarus during the time they had spent together, he even felt sorry for him in a way being an only child dealing with his imaginative mother.

It may have been the effect of the whiskey, however, tonight Avenyx wanted to see the smugness disappear from Millerson's face. So without another thought, Avenyx got up off his chair and made his way over to Millerson.

Avenyx approached Millerson from behind so he did not see him coming, but he knew something was up when the crowd stopped laughing and faces froze with their mouths wide open. Millerson instantly stopped mid-sentence and spun around to come face to face with Avenyx.

"I have something to say to you Millerson Thact," Avenyx said, his voice filled with superiority.

"Do I not need to bow at your feet or ask permission to speak first?" Millerson replied, keeping the smug grin on his face trying to impress the crowd.

"I did not like the way you spoke of young Aquillarus Willamyst. He is much younger than you, I'm sorry if you got a little wet but the boy has a talent he was just showing it off."

"Why? So he can feel superior to the rest of us?"

"It is not about that Millerson and you know that. Although some have chosen to study abilities, it does not make them different from the rest. We are the same as you and should be treated as such. Just because he has talent does not mean he wants to be any better than the likes of you or me for that matter."

"That is where you are wrong. We are not all the same. They start off like this, showing off cheap tricks, trying to fit in with the rest of us, then they end up like you! Watching. Sitting in your own little corner, with the others too nervous to even speak to you. While you sit back and feed on it. You love it! You love the fact that most of these men and women worship you and you hardly give them the time of day. If I let him continue without putting him in his place now, what will become of him? I think we both know the answer and that is all this town needs, another you for them to all look up to. When he starts acting like the rest of us, then I will treat him like the rest of us. So if you're done oh great and mighty one, kindly take a seat back over on your throne, while the rest of us that work every day enjoy our time off."

Avenyx paused for a moment not expecting this reply and realizing he was not getting through to this man and doubted he ever would.

"You make it extremely difficult for me to help you Millerson; it just always seems to be a never-ending struggle with you. Sometimes I just want to give up."

"Let me put it another way for you...*God*. If I were covered in flames, you would be the last person I ask to help me put the fire out."

Avenyx turned at this and walked away.

"You know it would probably be one of your *gifted* friends that started it in the first place."

Chapter 8

The night was coming to an end as Ticcarus and Avenyx assisted an extremely tipsy Jenwa up onto the bar, there were only a handful of stragglers drinking, singing, or ranting at one another. The band of misfits that usually played their instruments and attempted to sing had left for the evening. Ruby had sent the other barmaids home for the night as they were no longer required, but Jenwa was always last to leave. Partly as she was the oldest; also, clearly Ruby's favorite. Once the other girls had knocked off, Ruby would allow Jenwa to accept the drinks the patrons would offer, which on a good night she would get fairly intoxicated, resulting in many of the men offering to escort her home.

Once upon the bar, Jenwa steadied herself so she would not fall, raised her fingers to her lips, and let out a large whistle that got everyone's attention.

"Last drinks Ladies and Gentlemen! Us Ladies need our beauty sleep," Jenwa called, which got a comment yelled back.

"You clearly don't sweetheart!"

Jenwa ignored the comment and got a hand down off the bar.

Being the first night of the four-day break, Ruby tried to stay open as late as she could, knowing she would get more business. Ruby liked to be present at all times during opening hours or if not, at least awake so if anything got out of hand, she was there to put it back in place. Ruby's was the only tavern around for miles as Hazy Foot was at least a four-day journey to the next town. People of the town knew a run-in with Ruby would cost them dearly. Having nowhere to drink, Ruby's was a safe haven and a place where you leave your troubles at the door.

As people ordered their last drinks, Ruby lent a hand behind the bar, pouring drinks, stacking away bottles in cabinets for tomorrow night and rinsing glasses in buckets of water. Avenyx and Ticcarus also helped escort those who had overindulged out of the tavern and on their way, they also neaten up the chairs and barstools. Avenyx and Ticcarus had to carry one man out the door on this particular night.

"We'll be back. Making a special home delivery," Ticcarus called, as he and Avenyx struggled with the swaying drunk.

Besides Ruby and Jenwa, the only person now remaining was Millerson Thact.

"I'll have another drink Darlin," Millerson said sweetly to Jenwa, as she made her way towards him cleaning down the bar. Jenwa looked over at him, rolled her eyes, then stepped around him, continuing to wipe down the bar. Millerson didn't like this and grabbed hold of her arm firmly. Jenwa let out a small gasp and spun around.

"I've done my last drinks call. I suggest you take your hands off me," she said sharply.

"I remember when you loved my hands on you," Millerson grinned.

"I remember when half the town didn't call me Home Wrecker, Temptress, Harlot.... need I go on? Now get your hand off me Millerson."

"We could have had something together."

"You are a married man, Millerson and very drunk. Let's not drudge up the past."

"I was married and drunk then, didn't stop you. Harlot"

"Don't call me that."

"It's true though, you wanted it. You still do."

"Get your hands off me!" Jenwa said loud enough for Ruby to hear.

"Millerson Thact! I suggest you keep your hands to yourself and leave my Tavern," Ruby warned.

Millerson slowly loosened his grip letting go of Jenwa's arm, Ruby saw this and returned to stacking away empty bottles.

"You don't need to be a Temptress to get Millerson Thact to do what you wish, just a woman," Jenwa whispered to Millerson.

"No man is going to want you once I'm done you know. Not even your all mighty God. You could have had it all but you had to open your big mouth and threaten to tell my wife. I sorted that out though."

"How is your wife? Still unable to bear a child?" A massive grin spread across Jenwa's face knowing this was one of his weak points. There was a time Jenwa thought she loved Millerson Thact, they used to sneak off together for days to their secret location. Millerson would tell her they would run away forever and have children together because his wife could not. He would take her to the broken watchtower where they would have their secret affair. That was until Jenwa worked out it was all lies. Hurt by this, Jenwa wanted revenge, so she planned to tell Millerson's wife. Millerson was not too happy about this and, because of his uncanny ability to get people to believe what he said, he decided to tell his wife that he was under Jenwa's spell. He told her that she was a Temptress charming him. Word began to spread a little of this but did not have the desired effect Millerson was hoping and did not drive

Jenwa away. Since then, Jenwa had not been Millerson's favorite person.

"Say it again Harlot!" Millerson shot back in rage. His face was bright red, the veins in his neck pulsed and he began to clinch his right hand into a fist then release it.

"Fine Millerson! From this day on I will be known as Harlot. But I will be a harlot that can bear a child," Jenwa said, as she turned to walk away from him, his right fist slammed against her beautiful face knocking her to the floor. Ruby glanced up at the right time to see this, instantly she reached under the counter, took hold of something, raced around to the opposite side of the bar, and stood beside Millerson with a shotgun she called 'Charlie' and aimed at his chest.

"Get out of my Tavern and do not ever return! Do you hear me!" Ruby's voice boomed. Jenwa slowly stood, leaned up against the bar with her hand against her face, blood began to trickle from her nose and the corner of her lip, tears rolled from her eyes, smudging the make-up on her face.

"She..." Millerson began.

"No one hits a woman in my bar. If I see you again in this Tavern, I can guarantee you I will be using Charlie. Now Go!"

"This isn't over Harlot!" He said, walking out.

"No Millerson, this is just the beginning," Jenwa replied.

True to his word, Millerson Thact did not enter Ruby's Tavern again for a very long time.

Ruby glanced over at Jenwa; once she was confident that Millerson had left she hid her gun behind the bar, wrapped some ice in a cloth, and handed it to Jenwa.

"Are you ok, my dear?" Ruby asked.

Jenwa took the cloth filled with ice and pressed it against her swollen face. She flinched a little as the coldness touched the wound. She had stopped crying and wiped her eyes with her free hand.

"I guess I should have seen it coming. I always did pick him as the kind of man that would hit a woman. No, I'm fine, the damage has been done. I guess this is what one gets for crossing Millerson Thact."

"While I do not approve of your escapade with the man, I do approve of you confronting his wife."

"I actually never got the chance. By the time I got there he had spun one of his infamous tales admitting to the act in a way."

"Well, the woman had a right to know and, in a way, I guess she found out a piece of the true man he is. I personally, however, do not believe for a moment you are a Harlot or Temptress. You help me out tremendously by showing the men a little affection now and then, give them a little flutter in their hearts, making them want what they can't have. It keeps them coming back for more. The more they come back, the more money they spend. I'm not a greedy woman but this tavern is my legacy and the only thing I really have in this town. I need this and them spending the copper here keeps it alive. I need you Jenwa."

"Thank you, I truly am grateful," Jenwa said, extending out her hand to Ruby's and holding it. 'I'm not sure though Ruby how much longer I can help. I will stay here as long as I possibly can. You heard what Millerson said, and you know he has a way with words. Although he's not welcome here any longer, I fear he will succeed; he'll turn people against me worse than he already has. I feel like this is the beginning and he has an agenda, I'm just the top of the list and I'm hoping you are not next."

"I'm a tough woman and I can take care of myself. I know my actions would have cost me a bit tonight. Millerson Thact does not scare me, he just needs someone to stand up to him now and then, put him in his place." Ruby had let go of Jenwa's hand and poured them each a glass of whiskey then pushed over a glass to her. Jenwa put down the cloth of ice and shot back the whiskey and returned the ice to her face.

"Thanks," she smiled, "I will though, you know."

"What is that my dear?" Ruby asked, shooting back her whiskey and pouring herself another.

"If the men of this town and Millerson Thact want to call me Harlot, I'll stick to it. Sometimes it's a lot easier to give in than to continue fighting, no matter what the truth may be."

Ruby studied Jenwa for a moment, she was not one to pry but sometimes she just did not understand her. She was so tough and strong on the exterior, and Ruby often forgot to think about what was inside, underneath the beautiful and feisty front.

"Why give in? Just be who you are, whomever that may be," Ruby asked.

Jenwa looked deep into Ruby's eyes, let out a sigh, and opened her mouth to speak but was interrupted by Ticcarus bursting through the swinging doors.

"Come quickly! Bring buckets, we will fill them at the well. It's Millerson's house. It's on fire!"

<u>*Chapter 9*</u>

"You're not welcome here!"

Gaidence was awoken by Ruby's voice booming, filled with rage and anger. Of the brief occasions Gaidence remembers interacting with Ruby, he had always thought her to be quiet and pleasant, this was a tone he had never heard coming from the woman. As he slowly rose, still a little groggy, he felt his shirtless body and cringed as his hands passed over the bandages around his torso. He squinted towards the tavern entrance at the bright sunlight shining through, trying to make out whom Ruby was furious at. He could see the silhouette of a man standing proud in the doorway. Gaidence was now sitting upright, he strained his eyes again, determined to make out who was this stranger that had upset Ruby. He could not keep his eyes focused long enough as his head was pounding. He turned his head away from the doorway to the center of the room where Ruby stood with her hands firmly on her hips and Leeif at her side putting on a brave front.

"Leave now!" Ruby warned but the stranger did not move, "Leeif, get me, Charlie. Bring me my gun."

Leeif glanced at Ruby and studied her stern face. He did not wish to argue or question her so instantly he ran towards the bar. As he quickly dashed behind, he ducked down for only a moment then stood tall again, clinging to the large shotgun which he threw across the room to Ruby. Gaidence focused his eyes as it soared through the air towards the elderly woman, he was certain it was going to hit her causing it to wrongfully fire. Ruby did not take her eyes off the stranger as the gun came towards her, she reached her arms to the side, then, as if the gun was drawn to her, it landed perfectly in her hands. She loaded the barrels, hooked it up on her shoulder, and pointed it towards the stranger.

"I said leave Millerson Thact!"

"I need to speak with the Valorgrace boy." Millerson barked.

"You'll stay away from the Valorgrace boys if you know what's good for you. Now go! You're not welcome in my tavern and certainly not welcome in this town."

"Aren't you a little old to be town Governess?"

"Nobody governs this town any longer! We take care of each other now, we don't need a scoundrel like the last town Governor we had. Poisoning minds with misleading information."

"I'll assume you are referring to myself, dear Ruby. Four eclipses since I've been gone and you still haven't replaced me. Does that make me still in charge and welcome in this town?"

"You know very well, that is not the case."

Millerson smirked his evil grin then turned his attention to Gaidence.

"Oh my, this one must be Gaidence. He looks just like his father, a young little Ticcarus. The other one clearly takes after his mother." Millerson said with his evil eyes staring at Gaidence. Gaidence bolted up, hopped down from the bar, his face screwed up as he hit the ground but he did his best to hide the pain.

"How do you know about my brother? If you know where he is please tell me." Gaidence begged.

"If you have that young boy and dare hurt him Millerson Thact, I will hunt you down and personally put an end to you," Ruby said, still standing gun, in hand with her finger close to the trigger.

"Ruby please, I do not have a problem with the Valorgrace family... anymore," Millerson turned to Ruby giving her a sly wink.

"If you have my brother, please do not harm him. Take me instead. He is still so young and does not wish to harm anyone," Gaidence pleaded.

"Why would I want to trade the tainted boy for one that is pure. I have no grudge with you young Valorgrace. Your brother on the other hand…"

"You give him back! You hear me!" Gaidence yelled as he started to walk forward.

"Gaidence! Stand your ground. You do not want to mess with the likes of this man," Ruby said in a stern tone.

"Yes boy, we wouldn't want you to end up like your father would we?" Millerson hissed.

"Enough!" Ruby ordered. Gaidence clenched his fist, his face went red, he was ready to take on Millerson, he was not afraid, no one talked about his father like that.

"State what you want for the boy Millerson, I have enough wealth to match your claim. Name your price for the boy and you to leave this town, like the terms of our arrangement."

"I hear your friend the God is back in town Ruby. I don't make it a habit of torturing and killing little boys that can see that which has not yet come to pass. Now a God? To rid this world of one of those, that would boost my crusade nicely. Prove that they aren't as indestructible as their followers might believe."

Ruby tilted the gun and fired it. The bullet passed Millerson's head, driving itself in the wooden wall behind him. Leeif ducked behind the bar, Gaidence stumbled backward falling to the floor. Millerson and

Ruby stood staring one another down with not even a flinch between them.

"Your aim is a little off in your old age my dear, best get out your glasses before you take the next shot." Millerson gave Ruby one last smile then turned to leave. As he walked away he called out, "He has three days, I'll be at Harlot's tower, he will know where it is. The God for the boy is all I ask." And with that, Millerson left Ruby's. The three didn't make any fast moves, Ruby still had a firm grip on Charlie, Gaidence laid on the floor, and Leeif slowly rose from behind the bar.

It was Ruby who broke the silence, "that man is pure evil, do not listen to him Gaidence Valorgrace, we will get your brother back."

"What did he mean about my father? Why has he taken my brother? Who is this Harlot and where is this tower?" Gaidence demanded. In frustration he glanced around for something to throw, when he could not find anything, he felt a lump in his trouser pocket so he reached in, took hold of what he thought was a rock, as he raised it above his head someone from behind grabbed hold of his hand.

"You're a little late!" Ruby yelled at the God.

"I'm sorry. I came as soon as I could, I was preparing for something and traveling by the shadows takes a little longer when you haven't done it in some time," Avenyx   explained.
The trio looked at him in confusion.

"As promised, in your darkest hour, or death of night. I Avenyx will be at your side, ready to fight."

"We need your help," Gaidence said frantically, returning the stone to his pocket. "I could sense this through the stone when you attempted to use it. It's what drew me here," Avenyx replied.

"Yes, how did you do that little trick of yours?" Ruby asked curiously.

"I gave the boy my God stone in case he needed me, I have a connection with it. It allows me to travel through the shadows to reach the one holding it if it's activated. In this case fear was what triggered it's activation."

Ruby was never really one to understand Avenyx's abilities, or kept track of what he could do. However, she was grateful to see him again and his assistance was certainly something they needed.

"He has taken Kendall to Harlot's Tower. I'm assuming you know it's location," Ruby said.

"Yes, please can you go bring my brother back. If you leave now, you could possibly catch him." Gaidence added. Avenyx knew of a broken watch tower on the other side of the swamp but never heard it referred to as Harlot's Tower, so wasn't sure of the exact location.

"I may need to follow him. If I confront him now, he may not take me to your brother. It's also a couple of days journey at least through that swamp."

"But please be careful, as he said he wants you as a trade instead." Gaidence was scared as his greatest fear of something happening to his brother, had actually happened. He knew Avenyx would do what he could to save Kendall, what he didn't know was what Millerson would do or how evil he was.

"Well, I hope it doesn't come to that, but sometimes sacrifices have to be made. I promise you I will have your brother safely returned to you as soon as I can." The God looked in to Gaidence's eyes for a moment and Gaidence knew Avenyx would do whatever it took to keep that promise. Avenyx then made his way to the door to leave the tavern.

"I want both of you back safely Avey! Do whatever it takes. I've lost too many friends which I believe are due to Millerson Thact's actions, I won't lose another."

Tears began to well up in Ruby's eyes, Avenyx gave her a nod and continued to the door.

"Until we meet again my dear Ruby," was all he replied as he raced off in pursuit of Millerson Thact.

Chapter 10

Gaidence marched back and forth across the porch out front of Ruby's Tavern, the soles of his boots clap with every step he took on the wooden deck. Leeif had previously completed the construction of the flower boxes and they were now filled with a variety of newly planted flowers. Gaidence did not take any notice of these and just continued to pace back and forth. Ruby made her way through the door, almost running into him as he was too distracted and hardly noticed her.

"I've made you a little something for lunch, please come in and eat," Ruby announced.

"Thank you all the same but I am not hungry ma'am," he replied, not even turning his head towards her, just looking across the town center.

"I did not ask if you are hungry. Now come inside and eat, you've not eaten or slept well of late."

"It's been four days. A full cycle from the first day of the moon to the full. Why has he not returned? He promised!"

"Well, it is a two-day journey through the swamp at best, not including the return trip. I know Avenyx would have made haste getting there. I cannot guarantee Millerson would be doing the same on the return trip. Millerson Thact is not a man who often keeps his promises. I am certain your brother is safe, Avenyx would have made sure of that. If Millerson does not return your brother, I know in my heart Avenyx will not let any harm come to him. Now come inside" Ruby left him and returned inside. Gaidence stopped his pacing for a moment, took one final look, straining his eyes to peer as far into the distance as he could. When he was convinced he could not see anyone approaching, he headed into the tavern.

They all sat quietly and ate their chicken and salad of freshly picked vegetables from Ruby's garden. Gaidence picked at his food, stabbing pieces with his fork, putting it back down then eating it. Ruby knew his mind was somewhere else as he constantly turned to the door then back with a disappointed look on his face. Ruby had finished by the time he was halfway through. She began to clear the table around Gaidence.

"My mother used to tell a tale to Kendall and me, when we were a lot younger, just before… just before she went away," Gaidence began.

"What was it she used to tell you, my dear?" Ruby asked curiously.

"She spoke of a time long, long ago. At the time of a massive storm, there were tornados, vicious winds, and rains that lasted for many days and many nights. This storm was so violent it destroyed homes, it pulled trees up from the ground, it threw large boulders around like they were a handful of pebbles. There was a village that was so close to the storm that it was completely destroyed, however somehow all the villagers survived."

Gaidence paused for a moment and looked into the old woman's aging eyes and could see the tears welling up in them.

"There was a man. A mysterious stranger dressed all in black, led the villagers in the middle of the dark and stormy night to a large cave. He led them right down to the back and huddled together with them to wait out the storm. Many were so worried, so terrified, they feared the cave would collapse. They cried and screamed in fear, all filled with so much sadness. The man promised them that if they all went to sleep, he would watch over them and wake them when the storm had passed. They were grateful but they were too distraught, they could not sleep. The man told them 'you have my word and I will do what I can to aid you with resting.' They wished they believed the man could do this as many were so tired, however, even though they all doubted him, he did as promised and kept his word. He sang them a lullaby and within moments all the villagers fell to sleep. The storm hit the village on the third day of the blue moon, the villagers awoke again on the last day of its cycle. They slept for four whole days and nights, without waking once through what was one of the biggest storms Thera has ever had. The man watched over them the entire time. When they awoke, they asked the man his name, he replied 'Avenyx'. One of the villagers spoke up and replied, 'No sir, you are Avenyx the God of night.'"

Tears now poured from Ruby's face, she pulled a red handkerchief from her sleeve and dried her eyes.

"My mother used to also tell me that very same story," she whispered softly back to Gaidence.

Ruby walked over next to Gaidence and wrapped her arms around him, "he will make sure your brother is returned safely, I believe in him and so do you."

Ruby continued to gather the plates and glasses from the table. As she did, she was interrupted by the sound of footsteps on the wooden deck at the front. Gaidence stood to attention and both fixated their eyes on the doorway. The doors swung open, a dusty and dirty Millerson Thact entered. He held a rope in his hand that he yanked tightly as he came closer. Shuffling through the door, struggling to stand, was a little blonde boy trailing behind him, covered from head to toe in dirt and mud. He had a graze on his left cheek and a cut above his right eye. The boy fell to his knees once inside and Millerson pulled a dagger from behind his back. Ruby let out a gasp, Gaidence's fists were clenched, tears welled up in his eyes, he wanted to scream out to Millerson but it was as if he was frozen to the spot. Millerson Thact leaned down to Kendall with the sharp dagger pointed towards him and sliced the rope tied around his hands.

"As promised," Millerson smirked.

"You're messing with fire Millerson Thact!" Ruby screamed in outrage.

"Trust me old woman. I know very well what happens when people mess with fire…" He stared Ruby down for a moment, it was full of evil. Ruby searched inside his gaze for a weakness, some sadness or sorrow but it was all gone. All that was left was darkness.

"…People die," Millerson said and left the tavern.

Gaidence broke out of his stunned trance and raced over, dropping to Kendall's side, he put his arm around him.

"Are you ok brother?" Gaidence asked as the tears began to fall.

"It's begun, Gade." He whispered, his voice so hoarse and his lips so dry. Ruby now rushed over also, "are you in pain boy?" she asked.

"No ma'am," Kendall shook his head.

"I'll get you a drink and clean you up," Ruby replied, returning to the bar.

"I'm so glad you're ok," Gaidence said and kissed his brother on the head.

"He saved me. He came and sacrificed himself for me. He made Millerson promise. He said that Millerson could have him and do as he pleased as long as he kept clear of Hazy Foot. He said if he included Hazy Foot in his evil plans and doings, Avenyx would guarantee every God and Goddess that ever was will come for him." Kendall said, now starting to get teary also.

"It's all over now. It's ok, I'll keep you safe. I promise."

"He's going to kill him, Gade."

"He's a God Kendall, that evil man cannot kill him."

"I saw it, with my gift. It was terrifying. Millerson Thact will kill Avenyx the God of Night."

Gaidence chose to ignore what his brother had just said and continued to hold him tightly, assuming he was just confused considering the distance he must have traveled in the heat of the sun.

Ruby returned and handed Kendall a large glass of water. Gaidence released his brother from his embrace and Kendall gulped down the liquid. Ruby also had a bucket of water and cloth. She began to scrub clean Kendall's face and hands.

"Your brother will need some fresh clothes, I believe you should return home and get some. You will both stay here for the night or as long as you wish." Ruby offered.

"I will later, ma'am. Also thank you for your offer. It is very generous of you, we would greatly accept it. We would feel a lot safer here, at least until Avenyx returns." Gaidence said.

"He's not coming back. That man is destined to kill Avenyx and the first God will fall to the hand of a Therian." Kendall said, almost screaming it to get through to his brother.

"What do you mean boy? Millerson has poisoned your mind, you mustn't listen to a word he has told you." Ruby snapped back.

"I wish this was not true but I have seen it. It came to me in one of my dreams. I know this as clearly as I know you will take care of me and protect me in this very tavern. A promise you told our father you would keep." Kendall explained as he looked up to Gaidence. Gaidence was not aware of this promise, he looked at Kendall a little confused, as he did most times Kendall told him something that he had seen or dreamed of.

"Is this true?" Gaidence asked Ruby.

"It is. Myself and Avenyx were close friends with your father. We promised to always watch out for you boys no matter what. Ticcarus believed great things would come from both of you. Although your father was not gifted, unless you count his kind-heartedness. He knew if he raised you boys correctly you would make him one day proud, which I am certain you have. He knew you would always be there for one another, however, if anything ever happened to him, he asked that we watched over you both. A promise we both intended to keep."

"I need to go after him," Gaidence said abruptly.

"Gaidence, no. He is a very dangerous man. You would not know where to start to look for him. Avenyx will be able to get out of this situation by himself." Ruby said.

"What if he does not choose to? He sacrificed himself to save Kendall to protect us all. He did it for this town he loved so much, so they do not return and divide or damage it any more than it has been. If Millerson has Avenyx he will leave all the other gifted alone in this town. If Kendall is right, which I hate to say, but he usually is with these things, once Avenyx is no longer here, what is stopping Millerson from coming back for Kendall and others like him. Why does he have so much hate? Gifted aren't that different from the rest. I'm tired of calling them gifted also. They're just people, we are all just Therian no matter what we are." Gaidence stood up, placed his hands on his hips full of rage. "I'm going after him Ruby, Kendall where did he take you?"

"I don't know Gade, I was blindfolded most of the time. It was dark, cold, and at least a few days away," Kendall replied quietly.

"You must have sensed something, seen something."

"It's a broken tower, that's all I know."

"Harlot's Tower, that's what he said. I remember him saying that. Where is this tower? How do I get there?" Gaidence asked Ruby.

"I do not know," Ruby turned away from him and continued to wash Kendall.

"You do not fool me, Miss Ruby. I know you know far more than you let on. If you are not willing to aid me, I will search for him myself. I will ask every person in this town if I need to."

"The Valorgrace stubbornness, another charm passed down." Ruby looked back up and smiled at Gaidence.

"It's not right you know," Gaidence frowned, as he pulled up a chair close by.

"It's the only way he would release your brother. Once Millerson was aware Avenyx was still around, it seems he and his followers created a trap Avenyx so willingly fell into. Millerson has not been around for quite some time; he would have had his spies watching. I guess we just thought Millerson had finally moved on."

"What are they going to do with him? I mean they cannot kill him, he is a God."

"I'm not sure what they will do to Avenyx and being a God will not save him from death."

"But…"

"When you look at Avenyx what do you see?"

"I see a god."

"Do you really? Remember back to the first time you saw him."

"I saw a man, a stranger all in black that saved me. It was all a bit surreal really but still, I saw a man."

"That's all the Gods are. Men. Women. Gifted ones, who have done a great deed with the gift they have. The only thing that makes them different is as part of their gift means they will not age, for this we look up to them, believe in them, and worship them. Why Avenyx is no different from your brother Kendall."

Gaidence looked back down at Kendall.

"She's right, we are not different from the rest and most like me chose not to share our gift, we just want to get by unnoticed and fit in."

Ruby smiled at him.

"It is ok, no one here will harm your brother for who he is. As I said, you are both welcome to stay as long as you like. My tavern has always been a sanctuary in this town for the people who need it. They feel safe no matter who or what they are."

"So is Avenyx really a God?"

"I believe that is also a question he's asked himself many times. Who am I to judge him or anyone for that matter. We all need someone or something to believe in Gaidence. What we call those who give us hope and keep us safe, is up to us."

Gaidence sat in silence for a moment trying to process this. He was not sure what to think of it all, is Avenyx just another normal person? He does always go on about how he is not that different from anyone else. He is right though, we are all different and but we should not out cast or single out one another.

"I want to go find him, Ruby. Where are they holding him?"

"It's a dangerous decision you are making and one that should not be made lightly."

"I know."

"It's one you should not do alone. However, if you are certain…"

"I am."

'"I am not aware of the location. However, I know someone who may be able to help you with that. She has also not been seen for some time, I'm honestly not sure if she is still around or moved on."

Gaidence leaned in eager to know more.

"Do you remember a woman who used to live in this town? So beautiful; always looked her best and men would drop anything to help her or even just to get her to smile at them."

Gaidence slowly edged back, he remembered a story he heard once about such a beautiful woman, the old man who used to run the Bread Store told men to stay clear of her. Gaidence face slowly changed and became filled with concern.

"I am guessing by your reaction you have heard of this woman?"

"I may have but isn't she..."

"You do still want to save Avenyx do you not?"

"Yes, ma'am."

"Then I suggest you seek her out, I believe once she lived on the edge of the swamp to the north of here, this home once belonged to the Valorgrace family. Someone in your family must have trusted her, treated her like a friend and most of all knew who she really was."

"How will I know how to find her?"

"You'll know her house when you see it and there aren't many people who live near the swamp anymore. Be cautious as many will have different opinions of her and will tell you tales that may have you second-guessing yourself."

"Is she... gifted in a way?"

"Are you judging before you have even met the woman?"

"No ma'am," Gaidence replied shaking his head, "It's just..."

"The choice is yours Gaidence if you choose to seek her out, advise her Avenyx is in danger and has been taken by Millerson Thact. She has unfinished business with this man, even after all this time, I'm sure revenge would still be something she is seeking and I'm certain she will have ways to find him."

"Thank you. I am really grateful for all you have done and willing to do for my brother and I. I shall leave tomorrow, please watch over him while I'm gone. Kendall, you stay with Ruby you will be safe here I promise, I have to do this."

"I know you do Gade, just be careful. As what you think you are really searching for, you may not want to find."

"The woman? What was her name?"

Ruby took a deep breath, closed her eyes for a moment, when she opened them again a look of pain now filled them.

"The people of this town now know her as Harlot, that is the name she has taken."

Thinking nothing of it, Gaidence gave Ruby a little smile.

"Take your brother upstairs he probably needs to sleep for a while. The third door on the right is empty. If you need anything come down and help yourself, just stay away from the alcohol." Ruby grinned. She helped Kendall to his feet and both boys headed upstairs.

Ruby sat alone in her tavern for a moment and played with her golden necklace between her fingers.

"What have you gotten yourself into this time, Avey?" She whispered to herself and shook her head. She called out to Leeif who came running moments later from the back room.

"Be a gem and fix me a drink," she smiled at him.

"Right away ma'am," he replied and rushed over to the bar.

Chapter 11

Gaidence stood at the edge of the stone pathway that led up to the cottage, he was quite impressed at the glorious looking home, yet at the same time, confused whether or not he would find answers here. He tried to tell himself this was the right place. Ruby said he would know it when he saw it and there was no other house or dwelling near the edge of the swamp that he came across. Well, none that looked habitable. This was not what he anticipated, he was expecting more like a lair of sorts. He only had the stories he heard over the years to go by. Before that, he was not aware of what a Temptress was. He had done a little looking into this woman before leaving and asked people in town if they knew of a woman known as Harlot. Some of the stories he had been told made him question himself as a man. Gaidence had always been so proper and the perfect gentleman, he never imagined a woman would perform such acts and especially in such places from what he had heard. Gaidence thought he would wait until he was in love, happy, and comfortable with a person before he would experience such types of pleasures. He certainly did not want some woman placing him under a spell to steal those moments from him. It frightened him a little, leaving him rattled; however, he was a determined man and he felt he owed it to Avenyx for saving his brother. He wanted to find and rescue him, no matter the cost.

Harlot's home from the exterior was extremely well kept, freshly painted, and refined. Although it was situated in a corner surrounded by swampland, it stood out from the gloomy dark, and dank vicinity. Along either side of the stone pathway up to the door grew a variety of brightly colored vibrant flowers, lining the walkway with wild reds, golden yellows, sapphire blues, and the most amazing pinks and purples. Each flower had been evenly spaced apart and carefully planted. Closer to the cottage, Gaidence could see an array of flowerbeds and herb gardens all flourishing. What caught his eye in the center of her garden was a giant apple tree, blooming with fruit. The cottage itself was made of a fine strong wooden timber, the cut-out windows all had floral curtains drawn and tied back. Gaidence slowly made his way down the path nervously and unsure of what to expect. As he walked, all the crazy advice he was given raced through his head, 'never look directly into her eyes', 'make sure she does not touch your face', 'as hard as it is to resist, DO NOT let her lips touch yours.' He paused and shook this nonsense out of his head, pulled a canteen of water he had strapped over his shoulder, and took a large gulp of it. As he fastened the lid and slung the canteen back over his shoulder, the strangest feeling came over him like he was being watched. He glanced around, quickly scouring the garden then looked over to the swamp to see if he could find who or what may be watching him. He convinced himself he was paranoid and marched up to the front door. As he stood in front of the wooden door, he admired the great artwork painted upon it. Brightly painted flowers around the edging with a large purple orchid painted in the center. He smiled to himself impressed by the details then raised his hand to knock on the door, however, before he got the chance to do so, the door flung wide open.

Startled, Gaidence stumbled back from the door then gazed up at the woman that now stood in the doorway before him. Out of all the rumors and stories the folk of Hazy Foot had shared with him, the main thing they had said was correct. The woman, the Temptress, the one that goes by the name Harlot was the most beautiful and elegant woman Gaidence had ever laid eyes on. He used to think his mother was beautiful when he was young until he laid eyes on Melinda and fell in love with her. Since she moved away, Gaidence never looked at another woman thinking she was as beautiful until today.

Harlot stood at least a head taller than Gaidence, she was tall and thin, and she wore a deep purple long-sleeved gown with a black floral pattern that ran through it. Her long dark brown, almost black, curly hair sat to one side of her soft face. Her skin was so clear and not a sign of aging could be seen. Her eyes were such a deep blue that just stared like they were frozen and fixed on Gaidence's.

"You're a lot younger than the men that come knocking at my door, boy." When she spoke, it was so soft and sweet, she even smiled as the words came from her soft full red lips. Gaidence didn't reply at first, he just stood staring into her eyes with a grin across his face, he felt like he was in a trance then it hit him, maybe he was and he instantly moved his eyes away and fixed them on his brown boots not wanting to look up.

When he spoke, the words came out quickly and nervously, "Ever so sorry to disturb you, ma'am, I am seeking your aid and hoping you will be able to assist me if possible. I believe you may know how to get to the location, it's an old broken watchtower as I am trying to locate a man known as Millerson Thact."

Instantly the sweet and kind expression dropped from Harlot's face, she lunged towards Gaidence and slammed his body against the outside wall of the wooden cottage. She retrieved a large sharp dagger from the sleeve of her gown then scratched it against Gaidence's face, which drew a trickle of blood that ran down his left cheek. She then thrust the blade towards his throat, stopping just as it contacted his skin but not drawing any blood this time. Gaidence trembled, unable to comprehend how the sweet and beautiful woman that had answered the door, transformed into a killer who had him at knifepoint within the blink of an eye. Sweat had formed over Gaidence's brow and goosebumps ran over his entire body. He wanted to gulp but was afraid that if he did, the cold blade would slice his throat open.

Harlot began to speak and the innocence was now replaced with a more serious and stern tone.

"Let me get one thing clear. You mention that name again in my presence and I will not just scratch your face. I *WILL* tear your throat open. Understood?"

Gaidence could not help but to gulp at this but luckily the blade did not pierce his skin; too terrified to speak, he replied with a nod.

"That man destroyed me. He drove me away from my town, made me out to be a killer, and much, much more that I am positive you've heard of. If you are a friend or acquaintance of him, do yourself a favor and tell me now so I can finish you off and make it less painful for you. This will be far less than the death he deserves and has coming to him. I strongly suggest you speak quickly and explain why you seek this monster before I get bored and decide to kill you for fun anyway."

Gaidence thought quickly of what he needed to say, the tale he had to tell was quite long and involved, however, he hoped the main fact would get Harlot on his side, so he opened his mouth and said three words. "He has Avenyx."

The dagger dropped to the ground instantly, as it did Gaidence moved his feet so it would not go through them. Harlot slowly stepped away shaking her head.

"You best be telling me the truth. Swear to me on your mother's sweet life, bless her soul, that this is not some sort of fabrication."

"I swear to you on her life, my brothers and the Gods themselves. The man that fills you with so much hatred, has the man we need to save Hazy Foot, the town you once loved. He has Avenyx the God of Night and is holding him at the broken watchtower where he plans to kill him."

Gaidence took his chances, raised his gaze, and looked into Harlot's eyes which were now filled with so much sadness that he could see tears welling up inside. She had one question for him that he knew was coming and he was a little afraid to tell her but he waited patiently and before long she asked it.

"How?"

"My younger brother Kendall..." is all he got out before Harlot cut him off.

"Kendall? Kendall Valorgrace?"

Gaidence just nodded.

"You're Gaidence Valorgrace? You're Tic's oldest son?"

"Yes, ma'am."

"Don't call me ma'am! It makes me feel old."

Gaidence nodded again.

"Please do go on."

"Mill... He kidnapped Kendall as Kendall has a gift. To release him, his condition was that we give him Avenyx. Once Avenyx got news of this, he sacrificed himself to save my brother."

"Of course he would. He vowed to protect you boys, for Tic, he would never let anything happen to either of you. Especially against the likes of Millerson Thact. Why would you assume he would kill Avenyx? He is a God or so many say, I'm sure he wouldn't let it come to that."

"My brother has seen it. Kendall's gift is the ability to see things that have not yet come to pass."

A grin formed across Harlot's face.

"Of course." Harlot nodded.

"You seem very confident all of the sudden and I have not told all I have to tell."

"I believe you. Although I did not know who your brother was at the time, I have watched over him, like I have for most of those with gifts who care not to share them with the world. Please come inside, we can discuss what we plan to do about Millerson Thact."

Harlot strutted through the swinging doors, entering Ruby's behind Gaidence. A couple sat at the bar having a drink and laughing at one another, when the man opened his mouth wide, staring at Harlot as she entered. He attempted to put his glass back down on the bar but as he could not take his eyes off the vision of beauty before him, he missed and the glass shattered on the floor. Leeif rushed around, also drawn in by Harlot's glamour, and assisted to clean up the spill, glancing back up at Harlot now and then not saying a word.

Gaidence was a little taken back by the fact that these men were paying her so much attention, does it just ooze from her then she picks who she wants to put under her spell? he thought or was it because she is so attractive they could help themselves at the mere sight of her. He admitted to himself he also had the same reaction and did need to remind himself to look away. Also, the whole time from meeting her, he has tried to make very little eye contact as possible, just to be on the safe side.

It wasn't until the woman at the bar noticed Harlot that someone said something.

At first, she looked up at her shaking her head then looked away but something made the woman go back for a double-take, something familiar about Harlot that she recognized. Then it hit her who had just entered Ruby's, proud as punch, daring to show her face again.

"We're going!"' She sternly said, telling her husband, grabbing hold of his wrist, practically dragging him off the barstool. As she dragged him past Harlot his eyes are still glued on her, the woman snickers, "He's still a young boy. Have some decency." Just as the couple reached the door Harlot turns to the woman.

"Even younger men just can't resist." Harlot grinned at the woman then give Gaidence a little wink.

"Leeif, where are Kendall and Ruby?" Gaidence asked. Leeif, still picking up pieces of glass and placing them into a bucket, sunk glances at Harlot. He looked at Gaidence as if he just realized that he was also there.

"Leeif?" Gaidence repeated.

"Oh sorry, Master Gaidence, the lady and your brother are out the back. Shall I fetch them for you?"

"No need." Ruby bellowed as she appeared through a doorway at the back of the tavern. She took a moment, looked Harlot up and down, then walked a little closer into the center of the room.

"If you've come for your job back, I filled that position many moons ago," Ruby said seriously looking at Harlot then a smile slowly spread across her face.

"Ruby, as much as I'd love to work for you once again, I don't let people tell me what to do anymore," Harlot grinned back then walked over to her and wrapped her arms around her. After the embrace, they took a step back from one another, and Ruby looked Harlot up and down once again.

"You're keeping well. Still have all the men drooling all over you I can see." Ruby flicked her eyes over to Leeif then back to Harlot, "Still going by Harlot are we?"

"I will keep this name until either me or that man is dead. Whichever comes first."

"So you are going to save Avey then?"

"Something like that."

"Good. Remember that is the real reason why you're going then."

Harlot flashed Ruby a fake smile.

"Care to join us?"

Ruby laughed, "My dear, I have missed your cynicism very much."

At this point Kendall entered, he looked at Gaidence and a smile instantly spread across his face. Gaidence walked over to his brother and scuffed his golden blonde hair.

"Are you helping out Miss Ruby?" he asked.

"Don't you worry about that, I will make sure the boy earns his keep. Your new friend can vouch for that," Ruby said.

"That I can, young man. I actually have something for you." Harlot smiled as she pulled a shiny red apple from the sack she was carrying. The others looked at her confused as she walked over to Kendall and handed it to him, "I remember they were your favorite."

"Thank you," Kendall nodded, taking a large bite from the apple.

Harlot placed her sack down on the ground and knelt in front of Kendall.

"Young Valorgrace, there is something I wish to ask you before we leave," Harlot quietly said to Kendall.

"I feel whatever I have to say will not aid or persuade you in any way. If you feel this needs to be done then so be it. Although I'm sure you will not let any distractions arise, however just in case one does, do not let anyone or anything try to stop you," Kendall said, looking deep into Harlot's eyes. She nodded, lent forward, and kissed Kendall softly on the cheek, as she did, she whispered into Kendall's ear, "she will protect you and I promise to protect him." She rose glanced over at Ruby then across to Gaidence as she made her way over to the bar.

"How bout a drink for old time's sake? Give the boys a chance to say their goodbyes," Harlot said and

Ruby joined her at the bar. "You're leaving today?" Ruby asked and Harlot nodded.

Leeif, who had now finally finished cleaning up the broken glass, walked around to the other side of the bar, still sneaking glances at Harlot when he could and fixed the ladies a drink.

"Anything I should know before I leave?" Gaidence asked Kendall.

"I'm sorry Gade, it's all too patchy, like bits and pieces that don't fit. The only clear piece is, he will die."

"Not if I can help it."

"Maybe you should not go, maybe this is meant to happen."

"I'm sorry brother my mind is made. He saved me, and then saved you. I owe him greatly. You know I cannot stand by and let all this take place because you say it must. At the very least I will attempt to save him."

"Millerson is not the only evil you will face that much I do know. Be careful and make sure you come back to me, we've lost too much already I could not bear to lose you too."

"I promise Kendall, I will come back."

Gaidence wrapped his arms around Kendall tightly and Kendall returned the hug.

"Remember why you are going, promise me you do not get involved in anything else. I fear this is much bigger than us, bigger than our town, bigger than a man filled with hate and rage."

"I promise," Gaidence replied, squeezed his brother then let go of the embrace. He turned from the others and wiped a tear that was forming in his eye. Gaidence took hold of Kendall's hand and they joined the others at the bar.

Leeif took another glass and poured Gaidence a drink; hesitantly he washed it back coughing a little as he swallowed.

"Get used to that burning it gives you inside, that's what will help keep us warm at night," Harlot said, giving Gaidence a little smile, still a little taken back from the drink he consumed and just nodded.

"All set then?" Harlot asked, knocking back a shot of some clear liquid that was in a shot glass.

"Yes ma'am, I mean Harlot."

Harlot shook her head and Ruby grinned as she took her shot.

"How are you going to survive with such a well mannered young man?" Ruby grinned.

"Ruby, do you remember who you are talking to. If anyone knows how to handle a man…"

"My mistake," Ruby sarcastically replied.

"Get your bar hand to organize the supplies I need round the back. Don't overdo it, we're only carrying sacks and we can't afford to be weighed down. Three days' worth of food and water will be most helpful and greatly appreciated as I have all the other supplies we will be needing." Harlot requested.

"Leeif, you heard the lady, get to it."

"As you wish my lady," Leeif replied nervously, then hurried out the back door.

"I will help you," Kendall called and followed after him. As he walked out the back door, he flashed Gaidence a smile that warmed his heart and gave him the courage he needed.

Once the two had left, Ruby walked around the counter of the bar, "I wish to give you one more gift before you go, it may aid you greatly."

"Trust me, Ruby, I've packed plenty of whiskey to keep us warm at night." Harlot smiled.

Ruby laughed, "I don't doubt it at all my girl, however, I had a different gift in mind." Ruby crouched down behind the bar and when she rose back up she placed her shotgun on the bar. Gaidence was a little taken back by this and took a step away.

"Ruby, are you sure? I mean I can't take Charlie from you." Harlot shook her head in disbelief.

"Please take it, I believe it may come of some assistance. Also, between the three of us, I know you have the courage to use it on a man who deserves it." The three stood in silence for a moment, all staring at the gun lying on the counter. "Don't be silly girl, just take it," Ruby ordered and shoved it across the bar to Harlot. A little hesitant at first, Harlot took a step forward and placed her hands on the gun. A shiver ran down her spine as her hands touched the cold metal, nervously she ran her fingers along the barrel, taking a deep breath, then in a snap, she snatched the gun from the bar and held it at her side.

"Thank you," Harlot said bowing her head at Ruby and Ruby bowed her head in return.

"You're a little quiet there Valorgrace, you sure you want to do this?" Harlot asked.

Gaidence nodded nervously and forced a smile across his soft face.

"It's a bit more real now, isn't it? Now that you realize people will get hurt and if they get in our way, they might lose more than a little blood." Harlot looked into Gaidence's eyes and for the first time, he did not look away. Ruby went to speak but stopped herself, she wanted to protect the boy and tell him he did not have to go. But she knew better, he was Ticcarus's son and would not go back on his word. Ruby knew Ticcarus would do the same for Avenyx, but Ruby did not believe Gaidence had it in him to take another's life if it came to that.

"He saved my brother," Gaidence said a little croaky at first then his confidence kicked in, "I'll do what I must to save Avenyx. Millerson is an evil man and if we do not try to stop him, there is no telling what he would do."

"My dear boy, you don't even know the half of it," Harlot said, as she walked over and placed her hand on his shoulder.

Chapter 12

Ruby shuffled across the open field, trailing behind were Jenwa and Ticcarus. In one hand, Jenwa carried an empty bucket while using the other to hitch up her gown. Not too far in the distance, she could see thick smoke rising in the night. Although they were heading to Millerson's house, Ruby was confident it was not the only house in flames. She could make out multiple clouds of smoke, it was as if there was a trail of destruction. At least four separate fires were blazing, each one further away from the town. As they came closer, Ruby spotted Avenyx filling up buckets of water at the well. Most of the townsfolk had come out to aid, equipped with whatever they could find to carry water, from watering cans to bedpans to help put out the flames.

Once the trio reached the well, which was a small distance away from Millerson's house, Ticcarus took over from Avenyx.

"Let me do this, my arms are strong and your legs would probably be a lot faster than these old ones."

"I agree with you my friend, however the further I am from Millerson the better we will all be. We had words earlier in the night, he was angry then, I can only imagine his anger now."

"You are here to help him. If he cannot see this, then he is more of a fool than you and I both thought," Ticcarus said, handing Avenyx his bucket and began to crank the handle on the well to bring up a filled bucket of water. Ticcarus handed Avenyx the second full bucket and Avenyx raced off to assist. Ruby looked around astonished and baffled as to how this could have happened. She was close enough to make out the burning homes, the fire did not spread from one house to another across the open fields. It looked as if each fire was lit individually, as she looked over to the next house up in flames not too far off.

"I'm going to make sure people are putting out the other fires." Ruby turned to leave then spun back around and looked down at Jenwa, who was kneeling down, picking up a bucket full of water. Jenwa eyes eventually met her before she nodded and Ruby took off. From a distance Jenwa looked over at the man who was not so long ago brave enough to strike her across the face, now sitting on the ground with his arms wrapped around his knee's sobbing loudly. She could hear him scream out on occasion, arguing with one of his friends who was telling him to stay and he could not go in. Suddenly it hit her. "Millerson's wife. She would still be inside." Jenwa was suddenly filled with so much guilt.

"Tic, I have to go in there. Someone has to go in there. She's obviously trapped," Jenwa shouted at Ticcarus.

"I know dear girl; those flames are still too high for even our friend the God to go in. I do not wish to say it but it does not look good." Ticcarus shook his head filling a bucket for a strong-looking man. A blonde woman came rushing over, she wore a blue silk dressing gown tightly fastened, her long blonde hair was set in rollers on top of her head.

"Marni my dear wife, what are you doing here? You should be home with the boys." Ticcarus scolded.

"I'm not going to be sitting at home warmly in our bed while my friend's houses are burning to the ground, thank you very much Ticcarus Valorgrace." The woman snapped back at him.

"How did you know? Did someone come to warn you? Are the flames heading in our direction?"

"Dear husband, the smoke is covering the night sky and the flames are so high. I don't think anyone in our small town would miss them."

"Jenwa, take Marni and some buckets. Head down to aid Ruby, we have more than plenty helping here. I'm sure other families need our help." Ticcarus ordered.

"What of…." Jenwa began but was instantly cut off by Ticcarus.

"He will not stand by and let her burn to death if he can help it. Avenyx will try to save her if he can."

Jenwa and Marni both collected a bucket, each and raced off to join Ruby at the next burning home, further away.

Avenyx raced through the crowd towards the burning home, the heat from the flames was intense as they still roared on. Avenyx placed one of the buckets on the ground, took hold of the other with both hands then heaved it towards the flames through what was once the window to Millerson's kitchen.

He dropped the empty bucket, picked up the other repeating the action to try and douse the flames, as he did, a young man came to his side.

"Is there nothing more you can do God? Please, I believe Mrs. Thact is still inside," He asked sadden.

"Regrettably not, at best I could rid the smoke, however this would provide the fire more air to burn up resulting in things getting worse," Avenyx replied, picking up his empty buckets. From above a black raven swooped over with a bucket of splashing water in its claws, it flew into the thick black smoke, hovered a little then swung the bucket until all the water had slashed out then it returned towards the well.

"Understood. I thank you for your aid." The man replied bowing his head running off.

As Avenyx raced back towards the well, his eyes glanced over to Millerson sitting by, distraught and tormented not too far away. For a moment their eyes locked on each other's, Avenyx turned away but it was too late.

"Is that it! You are going to run water like the rest of them!" Millerson called to Avenyx who ignored his comment and kept running. "Do something!" Millerson yelled out.

"I am Millerson." Avenyx spun around, dropping his buckets to face Millerson.

"Are you not a God? My wife is in there!"

"I understand…"

"Well, if you're not man enough to do something!" Millerson yelled, breaking his friend's grip heading towards his burning home. Avenyx sped towards him, grabbed hold of his shoulder stopping him in his place.

"You are a fool Millerson Thact!" Avenyx said, his voice boomed as he pushed Milleron to the ground then raced into the flames of the burning house.

Ruby stood on the porch of her Tavern with one arm around Kendall and Leeif by her side. Gaidence and Harlot began to slowly walk away with their brown woven sacks full of supplies slung over their backs.

Harlot held Charlie firmly at her side. They glanced back to take one last look at Ruby's and their friends faring them farewell. Ruby's face was stern, so serious, trying to hold back the tears as she feared the journey was going to be tougher than they both imagined.

"Bring him home safely," Ruby called.

"That's the plan," Harlot called back. Ruby raised her right arm making a fist and held it to her chest, "By the Gods."

Gaidence nodded and returned the gesture, Harlot stood for a moment just staring into Ruby's eyes from a distance, she mouthed the words 'thank you' then turned away.

"I'll be back, don't be worrying yourself about me, Kendall. You stay with Miss Ruby until I return." Gaidence called out to his brother.

"Be careful Gade," Kendall called back, which brought a smile to Gaidence's face and he turned to catch up to Harlot.

"This is it boy, no turning back now," Harlot said, Gaidence gave her a nod and they both left the town.

Avenyx sat tightly bound by a variety of different fraying ropes and rusted chains to a decaying wooden chair. The room he was being kept in was tiny and square in shape, made of stone. Although his mouth was not bound, he sat in silence not saying a word. His grey eyes did not meet his capturer's, instead, they stared off blankly out the small stone edged window, watching the radiant sun setting on an empty field.

Millerson Thact on the other hand stood tall, victoriously peering down at Avenyx from above. Now he was confident Avenyx could not escape, he advised the two men that assisted him tightening the ropes to leave and stand guard out the front of the tower. Once they had left, Millerson slowly strolled over to the stone window and gazed down at the field below. They were in an old tower left to ruin, which over the years had slowly fallen apart and crumbled away. They weren't too high up, however, if you were to jump out the window, it probably wouldn't kill you, but it would still be a painful experience. It was believed the tower was once used as a great watchtower in case of any attacks heading towards the swamps, en route to Hazy Foot. The men who were posted as guards quickly learned that it was a wasted effort and abandoned the tower. It sat alone in an empty field, that from the south, seemed to go on forever and the north was blocked off from the swamp that separated Hazy Foot from the rest of Thera, hidden away nicely. A good day or two's journey across the field would take you to Luccian, the closest town to Hazy Foot. However, the trip across the field was rarely done as there was no shelter or protection from the sun or the rain the entire way.

Millerson turned from the window to face the God bound before him.

"Not even a struggle. Not even a moan of pain. You didn't use any abilities. And you called yourself a God?"

Avenyx rolled his eyes then continued staring into the nothingness. Millerson pulled a sharpened dagger from his belt and slowly began to twirl it in his dirty hands, one step at a time, he made his way over to his captive. He was at arm's length from Avenyx with an evil grin spread across his face. Although Avenyx did not show it, he was repulsed by the smell of Millerson's breath. It smelt like he had not eaten anything good for him in such a long while. It was a mix of bad meat and stale gin. Avenyx wished he had some freshly picked mint that he could ram down Millerson's throat to stop the ghastly smell. This thought brought the tiniest grin to the corner of Avenyx's lips but it quickly faded as he maintained his stern no reaction look.

"Do you know what I despise most about your kind?" Millerson asked as his voice was full of rage, however, he did not shout as he was trying to maintain a stern tone, but not very successful at doing so. Avenyx kept his composure, not even a flinch when Millerson spat a little on Avenyx's cheek as he spoke.

"Answer me!"

Avenyx was in no mood to have a discussion with this man nor did he wish to try and reach a compromise at this stage, so he chose to ignore this. This frustrated Millerson, who slammed the non sharpen end of his dagger against the wall.

"I'm waiting, God."

Avenyx flicked his eyes to Millerson and stared into the deep pools of hatred then shrugged his shoulders and turned his eyes away.

"Your superiority complex. You and the other Gods, hidden, scattered around our world thinking they are better than the rest of us. All high and mighty. Then are your little followers and the "gifted". They're tainted, cursed. But because the Gods love them for being different, they get away with whatever they like. Adultery! Murder! Just to mention a few things!" Millerson shook his head and turned away but instantly spun back around to Avenyx.

"A God. All worship him. Believe in him. Avenyx the God of Night. A great protector. You've never done me any favors God, why should I believe in you?"

This got Avenyx's attention so he faced Millerson once again and just shrugged.

"Well now is your chance to prove yourself to me, win me over, turn me into a believer."

"Why would I do that Millerson Thact?" Avenyx said in a quiet and somber voice. Millerson was a little surprised to get a reaction from Avenyx and was not sure how to reply, a little off guard he took a step back.

"Please do enlighten me. You claim I have so much hatred for you. What would give you the idea that I would want you as my loyal and devoted follower?"

"Well... Well... I wouldn't anyway."

"You have no idea, do you. Just an angry man who has let his rage consume and control him. You are using one tragic event to win people over. On a mission of evil to kill a God. Really Millerson what is this going to accomplish? I've lived a very long time and faced a lot worse than you. You kidnapped a little boy; you kidnapped Kendall Valorgrace to get me to sacrifice myself. What did the Valorgrace family ever do to you? Nothing Millerson. What sort of God would want you at their side?" Avenyx eyes were narrowed, so sharp and focused on Millerson they could almost slice him open.

Millerson did not like this and slammed his dagger to the ground.

"You're not in control here God! I don't answer to you."

"Are you saying you are superior to me Millerson Thact? All high and mighty." Avenyx paused as he watched the anger grow as Millerson's face began to turn red. "How does it feel?" Avenyx grinned.

Millerson was not prepared for this at all, he needed time to think. He spent the last 4 years traveling to different towns getting followers, turning people against the Gods, to join his crusade for the purification of Thera. Now the time had come, it was not what he planned at all. He reached down, picked up his dagger, and took another look at Avenyx, "You're lucky I don't finish you now." With that Millerson began to march out the room.

"Oh thank the Gods," Avenyx sarcastically replied. Millerson picked up his pace, stormed out the room, slamming the wooden door behind him. Avenyx heard a large metal bolt on the other side be slammed against the wooden door and Millerson footsteps walking away. Avenyx shook his head and returned his gaze out the window then said softly "Eventide, come to me."

Even standing at the edge of the swamp, Gaidence could tell the atmosphere inside would be extremely different from what he was used to. There was not too much breeze around, and even though it was not a warm day, he could feel the heat of the sun shining down. They both stood taking in the view of green mangroves and trees intertwining with one another. There was only one path that led in, they stood before it peering into the green overgrowth. The path didn't go on far before it took a quick turn. It was a lot darker inside than out as the trees not only grew straight up but overhead also.

"Time to change. Remember how I mentioned packed loose clothing," Harlot said.

"Yes, I've bought a set. Is it going to be hot in there?" Gaidence asked.

"Not so much hot, more sticky, moist, with the sensation to itch yourself all over constantly but you adapt to it."

"Are there many animals in there? Like snakes and things? When I was younger, we were told never to go in the swamp, since you never know what might be in there."

"There is, but they are the least of our worries."

"What do you mean?" Gaidence was a little confused by this, having heard stories of a boy that lived in the swamp, and at night they would turn into a wolf which hunted down anything that moved. Or men that went into the swamp, ended up getting lost then turned in to some sort of creature.

"Did you notice back when leaving the tavern anyone watching us?"

"No, I didn't really look, to be honest."

"Millerson would know that Ruby would have roped someone in to save the God…"

"I wasn't roped in!"

"What I mean is," Harlot narrowed her eyes and her voice got a little harsher, Gaidence took this as a warning not to cut her off in the future. "We are being watched."

"Really?" Gaidence quickly dropped his sack, he turned around in every direction peering across the open field, and then back at the trees hoping to spot someone lurking in the shadows.

"Not here, we're in the open. Millerson's men clearly aren't the brightest stars in the night sky for following such a fool of a man. However, I feel they would have some sort of intelligence not to stand out in the open if they were following or spying on us."

"Oh yeah, of course." Gaidence knelt down and started rummaging through his sack pretending he had not just acted so rashly.

"I'm sure we will run into them soon enough so be prepared. Fear not, he's not the only one with friends lurking in the shadows." Gaidence jerked his head up at Harlot looking at her peculiarly. "A girl's got to keep some secrets."

"Trust me, I'm pretty sure you've got plenty I don't know about."

Harlot laughed at this comment, placing down her things and began loosening her boots.

"So why are you doing this? For me, he rescued my little brother, sacrificed himself. It's only right I attempt to save him, at the very least to repay my thanks." Gaidence began as he changed his shirt to a shorter-sleeved and much looser fitting one. "It's not only that, my parents, both of them, were believers in the Gods. Not that they told us we should believe. We were given a choice to form our own opinion, Mother always thanked them though, for just about everything. From when the rain stopped pouring, to when we recovered from a sickness. I'm sure wherever she is now, the Gods will be watching over and protecting her. I do hope to see her one day, it just all got too much for her in the end. She believed the Gods had turned their back on her, taking her husband, letting her little boy live in fear of his gift and then of course…" Gaidence glanced over at Harlot who seemed not to be paying attention and just standing there staring into the distance. "Are you listening to me at all ma'am?" He asked ever so politely. "Harlot?"

Suddenly as if awoken from a trance she bolted back to reality.

"We're going into the swamp to save Avenyx?"

"Umm, yes. Mill… he is captured. Are you ok?" Gaidence asked, taking a step towards her, reaching out to place his hand on her shoulder.

"Don't be so silly; of course I'm fine I know what we are doing. So preposterous, now turn your back I would like to change and I wish for you not to see me in my undergarments."

"Of course." Gaidence stepped back, picked up his sack, walked a little further away, as he did the thought entered his head to turn and just sneak one little peak.

She was a very attractive and desirable woman, who wouldn't like to see a little more of her. He quickly scolded himself and reminded himself he is a gentleman, this would be extremely inappropriate, why would he have such thoughts, then it struck him. He must be under her spell and not realizing it. He needed to be more careful and not let his guard down. So many questions and mystery still around her that were going through his head. Why was she going and so eager? and Does it mean that much to her to gain revenge on Millerson Thact or does she feel she owes something to Avenyx? Gaidence pondered all this. She did not seem too much of a believer, there were often times he doubted this with certain comments she made. He was right, there was plenty about her he did not know, and this was a little concerning. The thought of asking her again why she was doing this came into his head, but he stopped himself from asking, dropped his sack, and continued to change. Once he was done, he waited for her to call out so he knew it was safe to turn around.

<u>*Chapter 13*</u>

You're not going to spread bread with it! Hold it like you're about to drive it through their chest." Harlot ordered as Gaidence stood knee-deep in the slushy, murky green water on the stream that ran through the swamp. He loosely held a small sharpened dagger in his right hand with his arm extended out in front of him. Harlot, who stood on the bank with her hands on her hips was not the slightest bit impressed.

"Come on Gade, you need to feel it," she sighed "I understand you wish this would be nice and easy but if you haven't learned already, certain things in your life are just not that simple. We're not going to rush in there, throw him into our sack then whisk him back to Hazy Foot, all without a drop of blood being shed. The reality of it is, people are going to get hurt, blood and tears will be gushing at some point."

"I know, I know," he replied in frustration, he closed his eyes and thought of an image that made him angry.

He knew it had to be something that really upset him, he had to channel it so it would help him overcome this. He needed something to give him the courage, the fight to do what he had to. Gaidence thought all the way back to the day he was informed his father had died. Instantly the pain and sadness all came rushing back. The image of Big Jonas came to mind, the stocky man in charge of the Mountain workers, he always wore a wide brim hat. He recalled Big Jonas telling his mother, 'I'm sorry Mrs. Valorgrace, there has been a terrible, terrible accident. We lost a couple of our best men tonight." That was enough to fuel Gaidence's rage. He curled his fingers around the handle of the dagger and tightened his grip intensely. He moved his right hand up until it was directly in front of his shoulder with the blade pointing forward. He squatted at his knee then leaped from the water landing on the bank right in front of Harlot's face, the blade almost touching her chest. He was so close he could feel her breath on his face, it smelled fresh like the rosemary plant that they used to flavor their meat from lunch earlier. Gaidance stood frozen, his eyes staring deep into the pools of hers. His heart was racing but he dare not move, he held his position and they both just stared at one another.

Harlot was impressed. Although she would not admit it, a little frightened as any closer and the blade would have gone through her, but above anything, she knew better than to show fear to anyone. With one hand, she quickly took hold of the dagger and with the other shoved him into the stream; Gaidence went down with a large splash. Harlot turned and walked away, "Good! But don't forget. Never let your guard down." Gaidence mouthed the words behind her back, as she had told him many times already. Although Gaidence could not see Harlot's face, he could tell a massive grin spread across it. Gaidence splashed around and got to his feet, retreating from the water, saturated from head to toe, also covered in a variety of green sludge and plant life that sat on top of the murky stream.

"I'll be sleeping with one eye open tonight if I was you," Gaidence grunted peeling off the greenery from his clothes and tossing them back in the stream.

"I always do, Valorgrace." Harlot turned back eager to get a look at him. When she did, she instantly burst into a fit of laughter.

"What goes around, comes around Temptress." As soon as these words left his lips Gaidence instantly regretted them.

Harlot's laughter stopped and a serious look came across her face, "clean yourself up, we should keep moving."

He wanted to apologize and to explain himself by telling her it was all in jest but Gaidence knew it was too late so all he replied was, "yes ma'am." He hurried until the majority of the green was all but gone and watched

Harlot walk off, picking up her sack, wandering deeper into the swamp.

They ventured on for some time, the more they progressed the thicker the air came. The trees and shrubs grew closer together and there was now a constant clicking or ticking of a bug buzzing around. They had jumped across, walked along, and trudged through so much mushy, sloshy, gluggy patches of what Gaidence could only presume was muddy water. Now and then a shard of light would burst through the gloom of their surroundings, Gaidence generally shaded his eyes when it did. He felt he was now well adjusted to the fact that he was the dirtiest he had ever been in his entire life. Even as a child he had not been this dirty, not even the time he went face first in a pile of cow dung when offering to be Mrs. Dellermore's farm boy to earn some extra copper. Then there was the smell, Gaidence took pride in his cleanliness, and at least once a day spent some time in the tub. Even if the water was freezing cold or he was too tired or too lazy to heat up some water to fill it. He would always soak himself either in the morning or at the end of the day and when he did, he would scrub his body from top to bottom. He was certain he was the general store's favorite customer. He would always be trading her cow's milk, herbs, or flowers for bars of soap the owner had made. And every time without fail she had a different smelling bar for him to use, he found it so cleansing. He was a little disappointed this was one of the items he did not pack for the journey.

Gaidence trudged on with a frown across his face following as closely behind Harlot as he could, now and then he would fall behind as his feet were aching and he constantly felt he could not take another step. Harlot turned around and noticed the unimpressed expression on his face.

"You're loathing this aren't you?" She asked.

"Yes," he murmured.

"Not what you expected?"

"I guess you could say that."

"The first visit to the swamp is always the worst. I guess many can't bear it, this is why so few come to or live in Hazy Foot."

"I just…"

"Go on."

"Can we stop?"

"Sure," Harlot laughed. She found a fallen log, half-covered in moss laying on a solid part of the ground where they would not sink and sat down on it, and took a swig out of her canteen of water.

"I just don't like being dirty," Gaidence said in a whiny voice as he sat next to her.

"Well, then I guess it's lucky you didn't get sent off to the mountains like most young men your age. Up there would be full of rubble, dirt, and dust."

This put the slightest smile on Gaidence's face.

"When my father came home, he used to scrub himself furiously as soon as he walked in the door, he also hated being dirty."

"You are so much like him, he would be extremely proud of you."

"Can you tell me something about him? To take my mind off things."

"I'm not one to bring up the past, too many bad memories. I guess I could share with you one of my most memorable moments of Ticcarus Valorgrace."

Jenwa raced back carrying two empty buckets towards the well where Ticcarus was still filling water for the masses who were putting out the fires. Millerson Thact's house was almost completely destroyed and the fire almost detained.

"Tic! Ticcarus! I need your help, come quickly." Jenwa called as she came closer. Ticcarus instructed one of the younger women lining up for water to take over his position and continue filling the buckets as he ran over to meet Jenwa.

"What is it my girl?" he asked, placing his hand on her shoulder while she gasped for air.

"Yellana…Her boy… Trapped in the house… We have to get him…" Jenwa gasped almost struggling to breathe.

"Who else is down there with you?" he asked.

"Marni and I. Her fire is almost out, so everyone is putting out the other ones. Help please." Jenwa quickly took a deep breath, made sure she was ok then her and Ticcarus took off to Yellana's.

When they arrived, Marni was still standing there, holding Yellana back trying to calm her down, noticing Ticcarus running over, Marni shook her head.

"You were meant to get Avenyx, he could have done something to save the boy."

"My dear wife, are you saying I am not as brave as the God of Night?" Ticcarus smiled trying to lighten up this terrible situation.

"If you're going in, you be careful Ticcarus Valorgrace, you may think you are brave enough but you're certainly not indestructible like a God."

"I'm going in with you, Tic," Jenwa added, and before he had a chance to disagree, she grabbed hold of his hand and dragged him into the smoldering building.

As they both climbed through a burnt out window onto a black floor covered in ash, Ticcarus called out, "where are you boy?"

"Help me," a faint call came from the back room.

Ticcarus turned to Jenwa, "all that is running through my head is, what if this was one was of my boys? By the Gods, I pray they are never in such a situation where their lives were in danger, but if they were I just hope there would be someone to come to their rescue."

"Ticcarus Valorgrace you are the noblest man I have ever met. I promise you this, if your boys were ever in danger, I would be there to come to their rescue. However, I can guarantee you this. No one would be able to get to them any sooner than you. You would fly like the wind, swim the great oceans, or even walk through flames for those boys. They are extremely lucky to have a man such as yourself as their father."

"Young lady, you are something special yourself you know. Hard as glass and pretty as a flower on the outside but on the inside, sweet as honey. I never did and never will believe a single word Millerson Thact and his convoy of misinformed larks said about you, and never will."

"Thank you," Jenwa said, smiling at Ticcarus, he nodded back and they made their way through the rubble to rescue the boy.

Harlot looked a little uneasy as she watched the tears stream down Gaidence's flushed face.

"I'm sorry," she whispered and he began to wipe away the tears.

"No, I'm ok, honest," Gaidence replied, taking a deep breath and trying to pull himself together.

"I'm just going to give you a moment. I'll get some dry wood for a fire, we'll set up camp for the night here." Harlot added and she got up and walked away.

Gaidence sat alone and sobbed a little more. He looked up through a gap in the leafy green array of trees above at the dark blue sky, he could tell the sun must be setting.

"I miss you father," he whispered.

Chapter 14

"Get down!" Harlot screamed as she ducked for cover herself under a small shrub. Gaidence scrambled to the ground, half slipping in the mud as an arrow soared over his head and planted itself in a nearby tree. Quickly, on his hands and knees, he scurried his way across the muddy ground trying to put his hands on the grassy patches heading towards Harlot. Once he reached her, he huddled up against her.

"They have us surrounded. Although there are only three of them as far as I can tell. What do we do?" Gaidence panted.

"Two of them still need to cross the water, which will slow them down. One was shooting from above, my guess, they are up a tree so that one won't be getting down quickly."

"Are you suggesting we run for it?"

"Not quite. Hopefully, we are hidden enough, if we stay quiet they might get tired of waiting for us."

"Why not use Ruby's gun?"

"The gun does not have many bullets; I do not wish to waste them. We will get out of this, I just need to think and this heat is not doing me any favors." Harlot seethed through her teeth and raised her hand to wipe away the sweat from her brow.

"Struggling a little? Do I sense a flaw in the exemplary Madam Harlot?" Gaidence joked.

"You sense nothing boy, it's just the heat that is all. And this is no time for that sort of zilly zolly, did you happen to forget we are surrounded." Harlot snapped back then peered through the bushes, exposing herself a little to get a better look at the attackers.

"Sorry," Gaidence mumbled and once again began scraping mud off his filthy trousers.

"I can't see them," Harlot groaned and as she did, a large rock came hurtling towards her, she swiftly returned to her hiding position. "It seems they have grown tired of wasting arrows or they're closing in on us." Suddenly as if from nowhere a gust of wind breezed through the area heading off as quickly as it came. Not so far in the direction where the arrows had come from high above in a tree, a man screamed out for help. Gaidence gave Harlot a curious look then scanned his surroundings. A whirling sound now came from the same direction, it sounded as if the wind had picked up dramatically in the area. In the distance, the screams trailed off and so did the sound of the wind.

"Get back from the water!" A deep manly voice boomed from close by. Gaidence scurried backward instantly.

"What do we do?" Gaidence asked Harlot who was already moving away, keeping as low as she could while she darted for cover behind a nearby tree.

"Move!" she instructed, and Gaidence followed, dodging another arrow that soared past his leg, almost clipping his boot. This put Gaidence off balance and his other foot became caught on an overgrown tree root, he fell face-first to the ground. Harlot reached out, grabbing Gaidence's arm and pulling him to safety. Once Gaidence was out of firing range behind the thick tree trunk next to Harlot, he searched for the voice that ordered them to move, however, something else caught his eye. The two attackers were crossing the muddy, knee-high deep stream. The water that once sat stagnant on top began to rise to form a wall of water in front of the oncoming attackers. It was slow at first, just a thin sheet of water. Gaidence could see through it, he could see the men on the other side just as amazed. The force of the water rising began to speed up, the wall was not very high but it went above both attacker's heads. Once the water reached the top, it would spill over, saturating the men below. It seemed effective in slowing the men down and little by little, the flowing water picked up speed, making the men struggle to push through the water.

"How is it doing that?" Gaidence whispered to Harlot who was also captivated by what was happening. From a few trees, away Gaidence's question was answered. At first, came footsteps, followed by a man. He stood a little taller than Gaidence wearing a long black robe, covered in dirt and muddy splotches, with a hood that sat behind the man's neck. What also caught Gaidence's attention was his hair; his messy mop like cut appeared blue as the icy cold water. He held his arms out in front of him and one step at a time he walked closer to the wall of water. Gaidence could make out his lips moving like he was chanting something but he could not make out the words. The rush of water was constantly flowing, now extremely fast like a waterfall. The men were fighting against the water with their bows, trying to break through but the current was too strong. The men struggled to stay standing as the water falling on their heads came down hard; they held onto one another's shoulders to steady themselves. Knowing they would not win they attempted to turn to run away. The man in the robe was now on the bank opposite the men. "Go!" he screamed, as he did, he pulled back his arms then instantly jolted them forward like he was shoving someone over. When he did this the wall of water also moved, as it was being the one shoved. The water took off with such a force that it rammed the men back deeper into the swamplands. Once the wall broke and the water dispersed the men got to their feet still dripping wet and fled, leaving their weapons behind which they dropped when flying through the air.

The stranger shook his head and as he did, the color of his hair changed from the pale blue to a natural auburn that looked similar to the color of copper. He walked over grinning at Harlot. When he was n front of her he reached out his arm to help her to her feet.

"You owe me one, sweetheart." He spoke giving her a wink. Harlot ignored his hand using the tree to help her stand up, she then leaned over and kissed the stranger softly on the cheek.

"There. Now we're even," she shook her head and he was grinning ear to ear, "you have my thanks, Aquillarus."

Gaidence still remained on the ground huddled next to the tree, looking up amazed and confused.

"You know him?" Gaidence finally asked as he got up to join them.

"Gaidence Valorgrace, meet Aquillarus Willamyst," Harlot rolled her eyes then began to brush herself off.

"The Elementalist! She never adds that part. You can call me Aquilla," Aquillarus smiled reaching out to shake Gaidence's hand. Gaidence took Aquillarus's hand, he began to shake it then instantly drew his hand back.

"Sorry, they get a little cold, happens after water. Just remember not to touch me after a fire, let's just say

I'm too hot to handle." Aquillarus laughed at his own joke but quickly turned to Harlot, "you can touch me though. Anytime....anywhere." He gave her a bit of a seductive look.

"We didn't really need your help," Harlot said, ignoring his last comment.

"What are friends for, I'm happy to come to your rescue, it's like you have me under some sort of spell, but I'm not complaining," Aquillarus said, still trying to get a reaction.

"We are not friends Aquillarus."

"Oh no. We're more than that."

"Gaidence, you will learn to ignore Aquilla's constant flirtation and attempts to win my heart. The poor man has been out here living with the elements for far too long, I fear they have affected his brain as I am almost certain he has forgotten how to treat a lady." Gaidence just nodded poking his hand as the coldness of Aquillarus's touch wore off.

"What are you two doing out here anyway? Or should I not ask? He looks a little young for you if you ask me, you need a real man. Someone a bit older who knows a few tricks."

"Someone like yourself perhaps?" Harlot said in her sweet voice and moved closer to Aquillarus.

"Seen twenty-six double eclipses and counting. And you know I can be as gentle as the wind or fiery as a volcano." Aquillarus closed his eyes and when he opened them again, they were as red as fire.

"No thanks!" Harlot shot back and shoved Aquillarus to the ground, "and that sporadic stubble you call facial hair, hardly makes you a man." Aquillarus let out a groan of pain, returned to his feet and his eyes were back to his natural light green color.

"We're looking for someone," Harlot said.

"Who?"

"I can't say as you will insist on coming along."

"What can I say I'm under your spell and cannot resist following you. Who is it? I could come in handy you know."

"Listen Aquilla, I don't want to get you involved. He's dangerous and if he sees you, I'm not sure…"

"Him!" Aquillarus said, cutting Harlot off, "you know where he is? After all this time he has returned, hasn't he? I thought our town got rid of him once and for all. I knew he would return. The stories he had told about me, about us all….. that man turned the town against me. I'm coming with you. I have a score to settle and you two could use my help."

"Stay calm," Harlot placed her hand on his shoulder, "I suffered the same as you. We helped each other through those tough times, however, there is more to our mission you must know."

"Why are you chasing him now? It's been such a long time? What has he done?"

Harlot just looked into his eyes; she could not say it. Aquillarus also has had a bad history with Millerson and believed so strongly in Avenyx since he had been so instrumental in helping him with his abilities. Avenyx helped him grow and most of all believed in him. Harlot knew Aquillarus would join the cause to save him and put a stop to Millerson Thact.

There was a moment of silence, the pair just stared at one another while Aquillarus waited for his answer, an answer that Gaidence delivered.

"He has Avenyx."

Aquillarus's eyes opened widely as he thought back to the last time he had seen Avenyx, ten years ago. He was also confronted with the memory of what took place that very same night, the night of the fires, and how it all began.

Aquillarus left Ruby's Tavern angry that once again Millerson Thact has resulted in him getting thrown out. He was just using his abilities he had been studying to get him a few free drinks. So Millerson got a little wet. Aquillarus didn't believe it was totally his fault; he had it under control until Millerson bumped into him. It's just because he was the youngest everyone treated him differently but he was mature, he had to be, he was an only child and his father left them long ago when he was just a small boy. Also, Aquillarus never had any friends. All the boys in town thought he was different because he spent a lot of his time reading books and studying the old art of elemental magic. As for the girls, Aquillarus always had that rough around the edges look, as he didn't put too much into his appearance. His hair was never combed, his clothes were always tattered or torn, his shirt never tucked in, laces usually were undone, and always had dirt or soot on his face. Just a tiny smear somewhere like he had attempted to clean his face but missed a spot. He was always thin and tall for his age, but the one thing Aquillarus had going for him was his confidence in himself. He used to constantly tell his mother he was going to master the elements one day. Although he could only do a couple of less effective tricks, like the water trick and make the air rustle a pile of leaves on the ground. Aquillarus knew with time and practice he would be amazing. He would show everyone especially, Millerson Thact that he was the real deal and a force that Millerson could not insult or mess with.

Aquillarus walked down the main street kicking small rocks with his feet, thinking about how angry Millerson had made him. It frustrated him to no end that Millerson hated people who were different, that Millerson was not so open and accepting. Millerson was born with no gift or ability, however, neither was

Aquillarus and this did not stop him, he wanted to be gifted so badly he searched until he found a way to be special. He would talk about magic to everyone and anyone, ask them questions, always wanting to know more. Many laughed at him, but he found the one or two that would lend him books to read and learn more. He knew if he applied himself to learning spells and quick incantations, he could become one with the elements, and one day control them. It was referred to by many as 'simple magic' and sometimes 'fool's magic'. But for Aquillarus it was enough. He knew it would take years to master and he would have to practice every day. But deep down he wanted this and was willing to make the sacrifice. Being so proud of such achievements and skills he had acquired, sharing them with others sometimes attracted the wrong attention. For example, the likes of Millerson Thact calling him *'undesirable taint'* made Aquillarus so full of rage, so angry like the flames of a burning fire.

Aquillarus stormed around through people's pumpkin patches and cornfields in no specific direction, it wasn't until he could see a flame of a candle burning lowly in a window that he stopped in someone's field of crops. He stood for a moment watching it flicker and dance in the darkness, hypnotized like it was working some sort of magic on him and he couldn't take his eyes from it. Aquillarus's eyes narrowed on the flame he pictured it in his mind, imagining he was the flame. He stared with so much control trying not to blink. He watched intensely as the flame slowly grew. As it increased in size, Aquillarus's concentration and anger grew with it; it was as if he was channeling all this anger to the flame, all that anger Millerson had caused. With a mighty roar, the flame exploded into a small ball of fire but big enough to set the curtains ablaze. Aquillarus was impressed with what he had done but then the thought occurred to him, the fire was now spreading and what if someone was inside. Aquillarus staggered backward until he fell to the ground, he scrambled to his feet and raced towards the house. He could see the entire house now catching alight as the flames began to spread. He took a good look and realized the house that he had set alight belonged to none other than Millerson Thact.

"No! No, no, no." Aquillarus said aloud, "this was an accident, I did not mean for this to happen." Aquillarus knew he had to do something quickly, he thought he'd run in, Millerson's wife had to be in there, he had to get her out. The closer Aquillarus ran towards the house the larger the flames grew, as if he was fueling the fire, he waved his arms frantically.

"Wind!" he screamed, "curse you, give me wind." He ripped off his shirt and began to use it to fan the fire from a distance.

"Please," he begged but it was not helping, he slummed down and put his shirt back on.

Aquillarus knew there was nothing he could do. If he stood around Millerson would surely finish him. He knew if he ran back to the Tavern to get help Millerson would be there and would not listen to reason. He could also not face Avenyx, the God would be so disappointed in him. All he could do was run and that is what he did.

Aquillarus ran until he reached a nearby house, he decided he would tell them he noticed it. As he got closer to the house, he could see a candle burning in the window. Aquillarus's eyes were instantly drawn to the light of the flame. Once again, just like what happened at Millerson's house the flame grew, much quicker this time, bursting into a ball of fire, setting the Taylious family home ablaze. Aquillarus sprinted as fast as he could but then something worse happened, it was as if the fire was chasing him, not across the fields but in his mind. He could see it clearly dancing around him, trying to aggravate him more. He reached the next home, there was no candle burning in the window he knew he'd be safe here. He ran up to it, bashing on the front door.

"FIRE!" he screamed at the top of his lungs, "FIRE!"

As Yellana Herringtor opened the front door in her soft, warm dressing gown, carrying a brass candlestick with a small candle burning low. Aquillarus's eyes met the flames, it bounced from the candle to the wooden door frame causing it to also catch on fire. Yellana began screaming, "What? How did you do this? Help me, my son is in here!"

Tears began to stream down Aquillarus's face, the tears came out as normal size tears but as they hit the ground, they were ten times bigger. It was as if they magically expanded like the water in the tavern. Aquillarus did not know what to do, so he ran. Images of the flames were constantly in his head torturing him. As he ran, he began to head as far away from anyone as he could. Aquillarus continued to run until he was out of breath, he hunched over, the tears were still flowing, still expanding before they hit the ground. He took a look at his surroundings as he caught his breath, he was on the edge of the swamp. In the distance, he could still make out the smoke rising. He knew he couldn't go back, not now, not ever. Millerson would surely come to the conclusion this was Aquillarus's fault, as he always needed to blame someone else.

He lay back on the ground and stared up at the twinkling wonder of stars in the night sky. His thoughts turned to Avenyx and wondered how he does it all, how he controls the darkness. The story goes that each star represents one that Avenyx had saved or aided as a reminder of how he helped so many. Aquillarus thought of counting them but there were hundreds if not thousands, Avenyx truly must have been so courageous and lived for so long as there were so many. Slowly he sat with his legs crossed, made a fist with his right hand placing it over his heart then he whispered quietly to the night, "by the Gods, please, please guide me." He closed his eyes and sobbed to himself. When he opened his eyes again, he could see his tears had made a tiny trickle, like a stream that led in towards the mass of trees. He rubbed his eyes to make sure he was not imagining it but when he opened them again, the stream sparkled a little in the light of the two moons above. Aquillarus took one final look at the thick black smoke rising into the night sky in the distance.

"Thank you. If I ever get the opportunity to repay this, I promise I will do whatever I can."

With that Aquillarus ran into the swamp following his trickling stream of tears.

Chapter 15

Avenyx watched on, impressed as the black raven pecked away at the rope that bound his hands to the arms of the wooden chair, he stretched out his fingers and twisted around his wrists. As rope still held him down, he could escape if he chose to but he was satisfied he could move his hands freely, making him a lot more comfortable. Avenyx heard footsteps coming towards the door.

"Eventide return home," Avenyx whispered, instantly the black raven took off out the window. Avenyx moved his arms to his sides so no one would notice they were now free. He then closed his eyes to pretend he was sleeping as he heard the rattling of keys outside of the door. There was a large click followed by the door creaking open. He half-opened one eye to spy who was coming through the door and was a little surprised to see a woman enter, instantly he opened both eyes and glared at her.

The woman wore what appeared to be a self-made leather outfit, looking like some kind of armor with a leather helmet tightly fastened to her head. Her face was aged and covered with dirt, her dark eyes were sunken back in her wrinkly face, she looked extremely fit for an older woman and Avenyx could just tell she was not one to give up without a fight. She stood before Avenyx with her broad shoulders; one hand was carrying the key to the door, and the other held a clay jug of water and half a loaf of crusty bread.

"If I had my way you'd be getting nothin," she said, in a husky voice. She walked up to Avenyx and before he got a chance to reply she poured the water down his throat. Avenyx gulped it down as quickly as he could, he was quite parched and could not recall the last time he ate or drank since arriving at the tower. She pulled it away as he gasped for air then she pushed the bread up to his mouth. He moved his head forward and bit off a chunk, it seemed quite hard to chew, clearly stale, however, he wasn't expecting anything at all. He thought it was all part of Millerson's great plan to just starve him to death. So he was slightly grateful to have something. He swallowed the mouthful then took another large bite and the woman moved it away.

"Not the luxuries you lot feed on I bet."

Avenyx just forced her a fake smile while he continued chewing the mouthful of bread.

"Too good to answer me, are ya?" She said, taking a mouthful of water from the jug herself. Avenyx swallowed hard then replied, "just didn't want to be rude and speak with a mouthful. Thank you, I'm very appreciative of your kindness."

"I ain't being kind, just following orders. If it was me in charge, you'd be dead already."

"Then I guess I should be thanking my lucky stars."

The woman shoved the remainder of the bread to Avenyx's mouth, he ate it then she gave him another drink of water and turned to leave.

"May I ask you a question?" Avenyx asked just as she got to the door.

"Can't say I'll give ya an answer."

"I have never met you, yet you would condemn me to death. Why is that?"

"You lot are all the same. I'm sure ya know Erudiya, your friend, the God of knowledge. So eager he was to help people find out more, be smart, get clever. My boy worshipped him, all that boy ever wanted was to meet him. So me being a mother, I did what I could and we hunted him down, and my boy was good enough to meet him all right. He turned my boy against me. Too good for his old mother now he is. He hangs around with the God night and day, probably lives in some big house with him now I expect. It has been twelve eclipses since I have seen my son last, don't even know if he's alive. I heard about Millerson and his story, how the

Gods turn their backs on us if we ain't gifted as ya call it. My son ain't gifted, but he was smart and must have impressed that God. You Gods took my only family away from me. Turns out I'm not the only one it happens to." Avenyx looked at the woman with concern but he did not get a chance to reply as she left the room, bolting and locking the door behind her.

"This area looks very familiar," Gaidence called out to Aquillarus and Harlot who were leading the charge through the swamp up ahead. They both spun around in disbelief.

"Gade, I'm sure we know where we are going. I know these swamplands quite well, I know every sludge covered rock, every tree from here to two towns over, I wouldn't doubt me." Aquillarus added.

"Oh I trust you, I'm just pointing out it all looks the same."

"We're not too far away from the edge in fact. Although I would recommend we spend the night here, this way we'll be fully rested before the attack in the morning. I'm not sure what to expect, I want a full view, no surprises from things lurking in the shadows and darkness of night." Harlot explained.

"I'm not too sure that would be the wisest choice, my beauty," Aquillarus added.

"Why would that be?"

"A surprise attack always works the best at night."'

"Either way, those men from this morning would have found their way back by now and warned Millerson of us coming. They will be expecting us."

"Harlot's right, no matter what time we plan to do it, they will know we're coming. During the day would give us a better vision to plan a strategy." Gaidence added.

"If you both support this strategy, I am happy to follow, let's camp as close as we can though," Aquillarus agreed.

Harlot started to walk off and Aquillarus stuck back with Gaidence, offering to take a turn carrying the sack. They talked while following Harlot who was pushing her way through shrubs, and swinging at insects that would fly past her head, the boys didn't take too much notice, they were too busy laughing at one another when Harlot came to a sudden halt. Aquillarus stopped when he almost walked into her.

"You ok?" he asked.

She didn't respond.

"Harlot? Is something the matter? Do you need water?" Gaidence asked, and suddenly without any warning Harlot dropped to the ground. Luckily the area she fell was soft and squelchy, but too soft, if she laid there for long she would start to sink. Aquillarus looked down at her not sure what to do. It was Gaidence who came to the rescue, he grabbed her arms ready to move her out of the mud.

"Aquilla, grab her legs, we need to move her," Gaidence ordered. He scanned the surroundings and noticed a grassy patch not too far away, "that grass patch, we'll have to lift her to there."

Aquillarus dropped the sack, taking hold of Harlot's feet. Slightly struggling, both men slowly lifted her over to the grass area and laid her on the ground. Once she was down Gaidence placed the back of his hand on her forehead.

"She is burning up. Give me a water canteen." Aquillarus did as he was instructed; Gaidence tore the short sleeves off his shirt and saturated it with water, then pressing them on her forehead.

"Does she have any illnesses that you know of?" Gaidence asked.

"Ummm…"

"Does she often get fevers?"

"I don't really know her that well. We've run into each other a few times and she's helped me out over the years. If I needed food or the weather was too bad, I knew I'd always have a place to stay, someone to run to. However, she was not much of a talker and I never outstayed my welcome."

Gaidence stared into the distance trying to concentrate and think what could be wrong with her, she mentioned the heat doesn't agree with her. Could it just simply be that she overheated or she's exhausted or was there more to it? He then had an idea.

"Your hands!" He called out to Aquillarus.

"What?"

"They can be icy cold, place them on her forehead."

"Gade, it's not that simple. There was a lot of water, the stream is too far away, the only water we have is in the canteens, I mean I can try, it's just... I'm not sure how cold they will get. When I use my gift, it's channeled, like the price I have to pay for it."

"You've lost me. Can you do it? It will help here."

"There needs to be an emotion attached to it. Water comes from a very calm and still place. I'll be honest with you my friend, calm is something I am not at this moment. I'm just trying to put on a brave face."

Aquillarus bit his bottom lip and turned away a little ashamed that he had shared weakness with Gaidence.

"Please try," Gaidence asked but Aquillarus did not turn around. "Come over here, I may be able to help calm you." Gaidence scanned the area and noticed a large rock close by and he headed towards it.

"Sit on this rock, there's a trick I used to try to calm my brother. He would often awaken in the middle of the night from terrible nightmares."

182

This caught Aquillarus's curiosity, he turned and headed towards the rock, as he passed Gaidence he raised his eyebrows unsure what he was about to perform. He sat on the cold hard rock and looked up to Gaidence who now stood in front of him.

"What are you going to do?" Aquillarus asked.

"Just put out your hands and close your eyes." Aquillarus did as Gaidence instructed. "Now listen to the sound of my voice, relax, and take slow breaths."

Gaidence squatted before Aquillarus and took hold of his hands. Aquillarus flinched a little and opened one eye and looked at Gaidence, "your hands are somewhat soft, clearly you've never worked a day up in the mountains," Aquillarus smiled at him.

"Pay attention and don't speak," Gaidence snapped back. Aquillarus closed his eyes and started to take deep breaths. Once convinced Aquillarus was concentrating Gaidence closed his eyes also and softly began to speak.

"Picture a tree." Aquillarus raised his eyebrows but did not open his eyes.

"A large, big oak tree, with a strong and sturdy trunk, in full bloom on a bright and sunny day. As you sit under this tree it's supplying you plenty of shade while you rest beneath it to keep cool. You have your eyes closed and you listen, you can hear the slow flow of the water gushing from a stream nearby. You can hear the little splashes of the water softly crashing against the rocks and pebbles in the stream. Now I want you to concentrate on that water, listen to its soothing sounds, and relax. Feel its cold icy touch." Gaidence stopped and opened his eyes as he could feel Aquillarus's hands becoming colder so he slowly let go. Aquillarus opened his eyes and they were sparkling icy blue.

"Thank you." Aquillarus smiled.

Gaidence backed away from him and moved closer to Harlot as he followed. Aquillarus closed his eyes and pointed one hand to the canteen resting on the ground, he began to whisper words Gaidence could not make out. Slowly, the small amount of water remaining came out from the lip and floated over to cover Aquillarus's hands. It was as if the water was swirling around his hands like a glove . Once both hands were covered Aquillarus opened his eyes. Then as if by magic the color of Aquillarus' hair transformed into the same icy blue as his eyes. He lowered his hands, placing them on Harlot's forehead, he held them there for a while then continued to chant.

He stopped chanting for a moment turning to Gaidence and asked, "Can you feel her head for me?" Gaidence did not move at first, his eyes were just locked on to Aquillarus, entranced again by his transformation.

"You will need to check for me, Gade. I cannot tell the difference between hot or cold while in this state."

"Oh... sorry, of course." He replied, taking a step forward, he knelt down and placed his hand just above

Aquillarus' on Harlot's head. He could tell the fever was dropping; it was still a little warm but nowhere near as hot as moments ago.

"She should be fine. Thank you." Gaidence said looking at Aquillarus strangely.

"Are you ok?" Aquillarus asked with a smile.

"I'm fine," Gaidence replied as he stood again.

"Do I scare you a little? Being all different and looking all different?"

"I don't think it's fear, I mean my brother has a gift. It's just... well... you can't see his gift. I'm not used to the transformation is all. I like it, it's a neat little bonus I guess."

Aquillarus closed his eyes, shook his head, the color from his hair and eyes instantly faded.

"You didn't need to do that," Gaidence said.

"I really don't mind. I don't want to make you feel uncomfortable." Aquillarus smiled as he took his hands off Harlot's head and just sat beside her.

"It's just me thinking. At first, it was an adjustment but it makes me smile I guess, it's so unique. The part it is, how everyone else must react to it. I can't help thinking about all the terrible things they must say, how they must act, the names they call you. Especially now, I never really used to notice it, the looks or comments gifted people got behind their backs untilrecently, with the whole reappearance of Millerson, it's heightened I guess. But it's always been there, even in such a small little town like ours."

"It's ok. I don't see people much anymore but when I did, I somewhat got used to the stares and the unsure looks. The little whispers between groups"

"It's so wrong though. I mean I've seen what you can do, you've used the gift you have for good twice, but still, because your hair turns a different color and I just felt on edge or differently. It's wrong."

"It's not your fault Gade, people react differently at first when exposed to new things."

"Why though? Why is it such a new thing? Why do you get treated differently to everyone else?"

"Now if I knew the answer to that question, I wouldn't move around from place to place. I like being by myself though, I don't need to explain anything to anyone and can just be myself."

"But you shouldn't have to worry about what people think."

"I don't."

"Yes, you do. You can say you don't, but you just did it then. You said you didn't want to offend me, as it was all your fault when I am the one who is being offensive by acting differently."

Aquillarus laughed.

"Gaidence Valorgrace, you have not offended me at all."

"I just don't like it, categorizing, naming, tainted and none tainted. What is the point?"

Harlot stirred a little.

"I admire you, Gade, if only more people were as open-minded and understanding as yourself."

Harlot let out a large groan, flicked her eyes a little then opened them widely.

"Needed a little nap did you?" Aquillarus asked sarcastically.

Harlot attempted to get to her feet but instantly stumbled back to the ground.

"You're not going anywhere, it's quite clear you need to rest, so stay put."

"Aquillarus Willamyst, you will not be telling me what to do." Harlot argued back this time taking it a little slower and got to a sitting position.

"No, but I will." Gaidence spoke up, "You may not want to tell me what is going on but I know very well it's a little more than the heat getting to you. Your head was far hotter than I have ever felt and Kendall has suffered a few extremely bad headaches in his time, it's the price he pays for his gift. Heat, dizziness, tiny blackouts, and snappiness…"

"I beg your pardon!" Harlot shouted back.

"I might be young as you continue to point out Ms. Harlot but I take notice of a lot of things. You don't need to tell us what it is but at least tell us there is something wrong so we can be aware and look out for the signs."

"Signs? Young Valorgrace, the only signs you should be looking for is the end of the swamp and a big tower. I sometimes don't act well with the heat, there is nothing wrong with me. The last thing I need is you two coming to my aid because I've become a little overheated, as it's been a while since I've been in this swamp. Thank you for your concern but it's wasted here, boys. Don't get too attached. We are here for Avenyx, remember not a group of friends off on a fun adventure through the swamplands."

Harlot forced herself to get to her feet and started to stride off. As she did, she spotted someone in the distance, she saw them pull back their bow, shooting an arrow that was heading directly for Gaidence.

"Gaidence! Get Down!" She screamed, while diving to protect him. As she leaped she literally landed on top of him, slamming him to the ground. The arrow missed Gaidence entirely, however as it soared past it grazed Harlot's shoulder, cutting open her blouse and piercing her skin. Aquillarus began chasing after the attacker. The attacker noticed Aquillarus from their earlier confrontation and did not stick around, he bolted off as fast as he could to get away. Aquillarus, confident the attacker wouldn't show his face again went back to join the others. As Gaidence and Harlot got to their feet, the duo crowded Harlot knowing the arrow had hit her. Suddenly they both paused as they watched the bloodstain on her blouse. Harlot raised her hand to the wound to cover the blood that was oozing out, but it was too late as both Gaidence and Aquillarus stared in horror at the black blood now seeping between her fingers and covering her hand.

Chapter 16

Ticcarus raced out to the destroyed home first, coughing and spluttering, covered head to toe in black soot and ash. Behind him more wooden beams came crashing down to the ground, he raced over to his wife still coughing and she patted him on the back.

"The others?" Marnie asked, and he nodded a reply. Suddenly from the rubble, Jenwa emerged with the young boy over her shoulder. She was also covered in black soot and ash, the onlookers could see she was injured and had a large gash across her arm and the cut on her lip from the incident earlier at the tavern had reopened. Once she was safely away from the house she laid the boy, also covered with soot, on the ground. She lowered her face to hear if he was breathing and luckily he was. He slowly opened his eyes and hoarsely said in a soft voice, "you need to get away and not touch me."

"Sweetheart, I just saved your life." Jenwa smiled back.

"You're hurt," he said trying to lift his hand, but he was too weak and it dropped to his side almost immediately. She looked at a cut on her arm then noticed her knuckles were grazed and bleeding as well.

"Just a little scratch, I'll be ok."

"You don't understand," the boy replied even softer, struggling more to breathe and he closed his eyes again. The boy's mother had now rushed over hysterical, "help him!" she cried.

"Marni!" Jenwa sternly called, moving her eyes over to the mother. Marni helped her husband to a sitting position then moved the mother away and let Jenwa help the boy. The boy's mother continued screaming and yelling words that they could not really make sense of.

"Can you still hear me?" Jenwa asked the boy, giving him a little shake. When she got no response she began to unbutton his tiny shirt and loosen his clothing. As she did, she noticed a black substance on his shoulder that she tried wiping away with the back of her hand. She then lowered her head closer to the boy again to hear his breath slowing.

"Stay with me," she said and pushed a little on the boy's chest to get the air into his lungs moving. The boy took a large gulp of air and opened his eyes wide. Jenwa gave him a wide smile causing her mouth to stretch a little and her wound to crack wider, making flesh blood dribble out.

"I'm sorry," the boy said with tears in his eyes and pointed up to Jenwa's lip.

"It wasn't you. A nasty man did that earlier," she said, wiping the fresh blood away with her hand, as she did, she noticed something different, even though it was night and only a little light, her blood didn't take on its normal deep red, it looked a darker shade. At first, she thought it was the darkness of the night, so she raised it closer to her face to get a better look but couldn't make it out clearly.

"I... need a lantern. Marni bring that lantern over here now!" Jenwa called. Marni raced over with a candlelit lantern, the boy's mother came over and wrapped him in the shawl she was wearing.

"What is it?" Marni asked, as she bent down handing the lantern to Jenwa but as she did, she noticed what Jenwa was so concerned about. Marni instantly dropped the lantern to the ground. The boy's mother had also noticed, she snatched up her son and ran off as fast as she could.

"Marni, what is it? Why is my blood now black? Is it the fire?" Jenwa asked, with tears welling up in her bright blue eyes.

"It's not the fire my dear. I'm truly sorry." Marni stammered picking up the lantern but keeping her distance from Jenwa. Ticcarus noticed the commotion and rose to his feet.

"What are you two women fussing about?"

"Nothing my husband. I need you to go get Avenyx immediately. I don't care what he is doing, you tell him something far more important has come up and we need him immediately." Marni ordered.

"Don't talk zilly zolly, Marni, what could be more important than saving Millerson's wife's life. Have you forgotten his home was nearly destroyed and he'll be lucky to bring her out alive?" Ticcarus snapped back in a stern tone.

"Do not question me now Ticcarus Valorgrace, please just do as I ask. Now!"

Ticcarus had only heard his wife use this tone with him once before and that was just as she started giving birth to their first son, so he knew it was extremely important and left immediately.

"Marni Valorgrace, you have me very worried. You tell me now what has happened."

"Did the boy have any injuries? Cuts? Open wounds that you noticed. Did he perhaps scratch or cut himself on the way out? Did you notice anything like this? Anything at all Jenwa, if you did you must tell me." Marni's voice was now getting more and more hysterical which frightened Jenwa.

"It all happened too quickly, I wasn't paying attention." Tears began to stream down Jenwa's face. "We bumped into something but he was ok. I even checked when I loosen his clothing, there was no blood, some black, strange…" Jenwa stopped mid-sentence and realized this situation was a lot worse than she feared. Marni let out a gasp, dropping the lantern again then covered her mouth, a tear trickled down her cheek. Marni was a strong woman; it was not often she would shed a tear. Rumor had it she went through the pain of childbirth twice without shedding a single one, so once Jenwa saw the tear on her cheek she cried out loudly.

"Just tell me! I can take it! I need to know!"

"My husband always spoke so highly of you, so I will be honest with you girl. I believe the boy had something known as 'the sickness', a disease that is passed on by blood touching. It causes your blood to go black instantly. The symptoms that follow after that come in many varieties and can come without warning…"

"How bad is it Marni? What are the symptoms? Is there a cure? How long will I have this?"

"'The Sickness' is something the Gods called it so long ago, there was no cure. You may know it by its more common name. People nowadays refer to it as 'Destined to Die'." Marni could not say anymore, her soft face covered in tears. Jenwa opened her mouth but no words came out, Marni reached out to place a hand on Jenwa's shoulder but she pulled away.

"I'm going to die?"

"Many who've caught it, have lived a long time. It may take many, many years." Marni cried, shaking her head.

"I'm destined to die? The boy, he had this? This can't be true, he looked fine."

Jenwa studied the cut on her arm and sure enough, black blood was now pouring out of it. She touched it gently with her fingers then pulled them away. Using her apron, she wrapped it tightly. Her tears were still flowing and she looked up to Marni in all seriousness, "What can I do?"

"Honestly?"

Jenwa nodded.

"I have heard the stories people have begun to say about you in this town. If they find out about this it will only get worse. You must stay away Jenwa. My mother used to live in a cottage on the edge of the swamp, it's now abandoned and needs some work done to fix up the place. I will take you there if you like, you can make it your home. No one knows of it and it's far away enough from the town. I'm happy to help you with supplies and food, you can even grow your own, there's plenty of space and good soil. My mother used to have the most beautiful apple tree in the front. Honestly, I think this would be your wisest choice."

"You are too kind but if I leave now, people will believe it's because of what Millerson Thact has said. I'm not one to run and hide, I will fight this and him. I won't simply give in."

"You are such a young and courageous woman, the disease will be a tough challenge but it won't stop until it destroys you."

"I won't let that day come to pass."

"The choice is yours to make and the offer will always be open. If word that you have this disease gets out, I am unsure how the town will act."

"Thank you," Jenwa said, wiping away her tears.

"You are most welcome."

"Please do not share this with anyone. Whatever I choose, I promise to be careful so no one receives this disease from me."

"I believe you. However, we must tell Avenyx, maybe there is something he can do. Or he may know of someone who can help."

Jenwa looked at Marni then looked away and stared off to the distance.

"I don't believe he can."

"Why would you say such a thing?"

"I don't truly believe he is a God. I believe he's just an ordinary man that knows a few tricks. I don't believe the Gods and Goddesses exist."

Jenwa glanced at Marni who had placed her fist to her chest and with the most horrifying look on her face.

Silence. No stream trickling in the distance, no wind swirling, no bugs clicking, just silence, as if the whole world stood still. Harlot did not know what to do, she tried to cover it but it was too late, she looked at Aquillarus and knew instantly her secret was out.

"Why didn't you tell me?" Aquillarus asked, in a soft and caring tone.

Gaidence knew something was not right, but really had no idea what was going on.

"Harlot... Harlot your blood is black," Gaidence said, innocently and moved towards her, he was instantly stopped by Aquillarus' hand on his shoulder. "What are you doing? She needs our help." Gaidence tried to struggle but Aquillarus' grip became firmer.

"You can't help me, Gade," Harlot finally said in a soft and sincere voice, "not even the Gods themselves can help me."

"But..."

"It is, isn't it?" Aquillarus asked, cutting Gaidence off. Harlot just nodded as tears welled up in her eyes and she turned away from the two, wiping the blood off her hand and drying her eyes.

"This is why you live alone? And why you don't get attached to anyone?"

"Please can one of you tell me what is going on?" Gaidance asked, now frustrated. "Shall I?" Aquillarus asked, knowing full well Harlot was in an emotional state. She did not turn but just nodded her head to confirm she agreed with this.

"It's known to most as 'Destined to die'. It's a disease you catch when your blood contacts another's blood with the disease. From what I've read, it turns your blood black instantly and this is the only way to identify it. You get extremely sick over time, tired a lot, dizzy spells, memory loss, and eventually…"

"Well, I'm not dead yet!" Harlot spun around as if everything was normal once again, "We need to make a move, it will be dark soon, we can't camp here and you do want to camp as close as possible."

"Harlot…"

"Don't Gade. I know what you want to say, I really don't want to hear you're there for me or if there anything you can do. There isn't. It's no curse, there's no cure. It's a thing. A thing I've dealt with for a long time. I've gotten this far and it won't take me in the end. Do you really think I'm the type of woman to let something like this take me out?"

"Enough of this talk, we've got a God to rescue," Aquillarus said, finally releasing Gaidence from his hold.

"And maybe then…" Gaidence said quietly.

"Drop it, kid. As I said, I've been down that path a long time ago." They collected up their things and the trio continued through the swamp. As she walked,

Harlot remembered back to when she had hoped that there was an easy way to fix everything.

Avenyx appeared before Jenwa and Marni, as if he came out of nowhere, leaping from the darkness.

"What seems to be the urgency? That woman is in an unstable condition and could die at any moment." Avenyx said abruptly.

"Apparently she is not the only one. Look for yourself," Jenwa said in a sarcastic tone raising her injured wound. Avenyx's eyes widened as he moved to examine the black blood.

"Do not touch it, oh great one," Marni said, reaching out to pull Avenyx's hand away, then stopped to bow her head at the God first. Avenyx just rolled his eyes.

"It is fine Mrs. Valorgrace, if it is what I think it is, it will have no effect on myself. Please go back home to your children or assist your husband. I will take care of Jenwa."

"Of course," Marni replied and placed her fist to the chest, "By the Gods." Then left the two.

"How did this happen?" Avenyx asked curiously.

"There was a boy in the house. He was injured, I was injured. I didn't know what it was at first, I tried to help him." Tears began to roll down her face once again.

"You were very brave." Avenyx moved in to comfort Jenwa and placed his arm around her shoulders.

"Can you stop it? Can you make it go away?" She cried heavily and placed her head on his shoulder. Avenyx did not reply, he just sat there and comforted Jenwa, stroking her smoky hair.

After a while, the tears stopped and Avenyx just sat with her, not saying a word until Jenwa asked again, "Can you help me?"

"I'm sorry, Jenwa." He replied, shaking his head.

She pulled away from him then turned and looked him in the eye.

"Why?"

"I do not know how to."

"But you are a God!"

"It's not that simple, you have contracted a disease. A disease there is no cure for."

"They all look up to you and worship you. They say you can do anything. Here I am asking you to do something for me and you tell me you can't."

"I understand you are upset. Honestly, girl if I could do something I would."

"Upset! I'm dying, Avey! One day I'm just not going to wake up, well that's the way Marni puts it. She said you could help me. By the stars what does she see in you? What do any of them see in you? What is it that you did way back when that makes you so special? All the tales I was told as a child of the great Gods and Goddesses. Would you like to know something *'God'*? I didn't believe them then and I certainly don't believe them now. You are a man Avenyx. A man that dresses all dark and mysterious that claims to have lived longer than the rest of us. People in this town say you have made darkness appear, saved them in the night, talks to a raven. People in this town say a lot of things. Why, people in this town say I'm a Temptress, seducing men to do my evil bidding, charming them under a spell, making them stray from their wives and lovers. I know how it all works. It doesn't matter what the truth is, all that matters is what people believe."

"Jenwa…"

"Jenwa is dead Avenyx, it's Harlot now. Harlot the Temptress who is destined to die. You play your role God and I'll play mine."

"There is no point in continuing this conversation with you any further. I may not be able to rid you of this evil disease but I promise I will help, protect and do what I can for you until the end comes for one of us, however it may be."

"As I said, people in this town say things. Doesn't always mean they are true."

Jenwa turned to walk off and as she did for the second time that night Millerson's fist connected with her face. Jenwa collapsed to the ground and Avenyx leaped to his feet.

"My wife is dead because the God ran off to be with his sweet harlot."

"Millerson Thact!" Avenyx boomed, as he clenched his fist and began to raise it, but in the distance, he could see all the townspeople who helped put out the fires heading their way.

"This is where your God is!" Millerson called getting everyone's attention and within no time at all, the people of the town crowded around. "He was with her in the tavern when they started and with her again while my wife fought for her life. Is this the true face of your God?"

"Millerson, I am sorry for your loss, however, it is not like that at all. I went in there risking my own life to save your wife's. I carried her out of the burning home to you. I did all I could, Jenwa is also injured, I came to aid her just the same as I did yours."

"Why couldn't you save my wife? They all look up to you. Look at them all. Do you know what they are all thinking? What a failure. He can't even put out a fire!"

"What people think of me is irrelevant."

Jenwa stirred a little then noticing the crowd of onlookers. Not wanting anyone to see her injuries, she instantly got up to her feet and ran.

"That's right, run my dear! It's a little too late for that, the truth is out now." Millerson called out to her.

"This is preposterous!" Ruby called pushing her way through the crowd to Avenyx's side.

"My dear woman, it is common knowledge you have a soft spot for our friend Avenyx. The point I am trying to make here is when I needed him, when his people needed him, where was he?"

"He was with his people!" Ticcarus also called, now joining Ruby. "He is no prophet. He is the God of Night, how is he to know your house is burning down? Why if he knew everything, he would know how faithful you were to your precious wife we sadly lost on this night."

There were whispers and murmurs from the crowd all watching the display of events before them.

"It's because of what I said isn't it?" Millerson asked, tears now welling up in his eyes. "I said I wouldn't ask for your help if I was on fire. What did you want me to do? Did I need to beg for you to use your abilities and save my wife?"

"You are a fool Millerson Thact. If you think I wouldn't come to your aid when you needed help, then you are a bigger fool than I once thought. I did the best I could for you, we all did. No matter how much I despise you, no matter how you anger me, I made an oath; an oath to protect whomever, however, I can. When I give my word, I mean it. Words can mean many things Millerson, trust me when I say your home was not the only thing that got burnt tonight."

"He's right Mr. Thact. That boy you got thrown out of Ruby's, if you did not burn him early in the night, he would have come in handy about now with his little water trick." Ticcarus grinned.

"I'm not the fool. You people are. You worship a man who runs buckets while houses burn to the ground and you call him a God. He was really quick to defend a tainted boy but when someone is pure, not a gifted freak is in danger…" Millerson started to trail off as he started to process something in his head. Each fire was individually lit, the boy in the tavern controlled the elements not just water and the God knew this.

"The boy is not here to help because he was the one who started it. This path of destruction has tainted written all over it, the God knows this and covers up for him."

"Outrageous! And utter nonsense," Ticcarus boomed, then took a few steps closer to Millerson and lowered his voice, "I wouldn't start throwing stones Millerson. Remember I spend all day up in the mountains where we throw boulders."

"My point is Valorgrace. You all say he is a God, but do we really need him if all he can do is… well, can someone give me an example of what he has done recently in this town, or for any of you." Millerson eyes glared at Avenyx who just stared right back at him. There was silence. No one said a word they all just waited, hanging on to every word Millerson spoke. "I thought so."

"I did what I could!" Avenyx screamed out, which startled Ruby, causing her to gasp. "I would help any of you people by whatever means I can, you all know that. I shouldn't have to prove myself or supply examples. I don't ask you all to believe in me. If I am not good enough to be your God then so be it."

Avenyx stormed through the crowd, Ruby reached out her arm to stop him but it was too late as he had marched away.

"That's right, run away also. It's ok Avenyx we don't need a God here. Do we?" Millerson called out and slowly the minds of some of the town's people began to tick over, as a few sided with Millerson and cheered out in agreement.

"Why even I could do a better job than you protecting this town. What do you say, friends?" A grin spread across Millerson's face as the claps and cheers of agreement became louder.

"You'll live to regret this day Millerson Thact," Ruby said, as she walked away with Ticcarus by her side.

Chapter 17

Avenyx looked out of the window peering into the distance as the sun rose across the empty field. He was never one for early mornings; generally, this time of day was when he was heading to bed. He was actually amazed over all the years he had walked the land of Thera, he never did realize just how beautiful the sunrise was, such radiance of brightness as the mass of yellow and orange raised and gave light to the darkness. It lit up everything from the shining green grass, to the grey rubble of rocks around the tower. The once dark night sky, now a stretch of blue reaching out as far as the eye can see. It was an amazing view that he had taken for granted for so long. A smile spread across his face as he sat there just watching. His smile faded as he heard the unlocking of the door and he turned to see who was coming in.

"How did you sleep? Hope it wasn't too cold up here for you, our supplies are a little low to be wasted on the prisoner." Millerson smirked as he entered the room carrying a one-handed ax and a large red piece of cloth. Avenyx chose not to reply.

"So Avenyx, I've come to tell you what I want, it's not too much of a request, rather simple I think. I want the Gods. All of them, gone. I've been thinking a lot and it's that simple. Rid Thera of the Gods, then the tainted, and with no one to look up to all of your followers, worshippers, believers, whatever you want to call them, they will fall away slowly. If they cause an uprising then we will take them out too. Purity, a pure land, and we will be known as The Purist, the ones who finally stood up against the Gods. If they're all like you and so willing to be captured then it will make my people's work so much easier. There are so many of them out there. Why I've only just touched the surface, even now as I stand in front of you, my words of purity are spreading. You Gods have made a fatal error separating yourself, makes it's easier to pick you off one by one. The reason I have not killed you yet is because you're going to help me find them, you must have some connection, a way of contacting them." Millerson stared Avenyx down for a moment, waiting for his reply.

"Your plan is flawed Mister Thact."

"And how is that?"

"I do not know where any of the other Gods are. I chose to outcast myself a long time ago, why else would I come to a quiet, sleepy town."

"You're in hiding, waiting for the day to come before you lot make your big move and take control fully."

"And what big move might that be?"

"You're a God, you tell me."

"There is no big move that I know of. We are not planning some takeover. We do not play sides, we do not do favorites. We just are and do what we can."

"You do! You picked her over saving my wife because you thought she was a Temptress, a tainted freak like the others. Well, guess what...."

"Millerson, I have no idea what you are talking about. This was ten years ago, yet you still cling on to a terrible incident rather than moving on. If you've waited this long to have some revenge on me for something far out of my control, I'm sorry to disappoint you once again but I will not be dredging up the past with you and rehashing old wounds."

"I wanted you gone. I couldn't stand how they all worshipped you."

"Then you were successful as I did not return."

"I know it was guilt. You felt guilty because of the fires and you couldn't face them again."

"If you believe it was I who started the fires, you are mistaken, also you know very well we were at Ruby's."

"Don't take me for a fool God. I know very well who started those fires and trust me when I run into that freak again, and I know I will. He will get far worse than what I have planned for you."

"You have no proof, and I'm sure however the fires began, it was not intentional."

"Does it look like it makes a difference? Tainted. That's why I got rid of the Harlot and also drove you away. I would have purified the whole town right there and then if it wasn't for one person in particular."

"The town doesn't need purifying. Remember our deal, you have me, do with me as you will but you promised you and this rebellion would leave that town alone. Because trust me, if you go near that town on this crazy purity mission, dead or alive, I will make sure you have more than one God to deal with."

"Things change, promises break. I'll take your life if I choose, as for the town, I'd be doing them another favor."

"You did me the favor also, I never liked being their hero, their savior. I didn't need that town as much as you thought." Avenyx now started to understand how Millerson had poisoned his own mind through so much built up hatred.

"Of course you did. You loved it. The way they looked at you, the way you'd come to their rescue late at night. Then there was Ruby…"

"You dare say one harsh word about that woman Millerson Thact and it won't be you ending my life but quite the opposite."

"Your biggest weakness God. The old bar wench herself."

"I've given you a warning, I would not push it."

Millerson walked over to Avenyx with a smug grin on his face, he waited until he was right up in his face.

"You're tied up, what are you going to do?"

Avenyx acted quickly. He raised one of his free hands and clamped it tightly around Millerson's throat. Millerson choked for air and began to struggle. Avenyx squeezed tighter, then with a mighty swing, Millerson thrust his ax at Avenyx's right forearm slicing it into him.

Avenyx screamed out in pain as thick red blood gushed out his arm. From out the window, Millerson noticed as the clear blue sky flickered and flashed to black for a moment. Quickly Millerson removed his ax taking a step back heading towards the door and the clear blue sky returned.

Avenyx's eyes were black full of anger, "Next time Millerson I guarantee you I'll make sure I finish the job."

Millerson turned to the door and called out, "guards! Get up here. Bring more rope and chains. Make it fast."

He then turned back to Avenyx, "you have three days to give me the locations of three Gods or get them to surrender themselves to me. If not, I will kill you, God, hunt down your Harlot, find that freak that murdered my wife and rid the rest of the world of this taint."

"You are sick, Millerson Thact. The lies you have told over the years have finally taken a toll on your mind. You have this grand plan and these fools that now believe you, but honestly, the whole of Thera will not believe you."

"They don't need to believe me, they believe each other. Someone called you Avenyx the God of Night once and the world believed it. Why is it suddenly different when I choose to give you all another name?"

"Did you see that?" Gaidence whispered to Aquillarus who he was laying next to him and still half asleep.

"Huh? Kind of, maybe. I don't know, can we rest a little more?"

"The sky. It went black all of a sudden like it was night again. It only lasted a moment. What if we're too late?"

"I'm sure it's not." Aquillarus rubbed his sleepy eyes and began to get up knowing Gaidence was not going to let him get any more sleep. He rolled up the large blanket he shared with Gaidence to keep him warm during the night and returned it to the large sack, he took out an apple and took a bite of it.

"We should let her rest a little more," Aquillarus said, pointing at Harlot who was still fast asleep, wrapped in a large piece of linen against a tree. Gaidence nodded as he walked off with a canteen of water and a cloth he had been using for cleaning himself.

"May I ask a favor?" Gaidence asked shyly.

"Of course you may," Aquillarus replied a little curious.

"Well, it's just that, our water is kind of low and there is not a stream nearby and…"

"Oh, of course. How much? Enough to get you through the day?"

"Actually… I really hate being dirty. I know it's just going to get worse but I also know today is a big day. Not knowing how it will all end, I would be much happier if I could start the day knowing I was clean or at the very least, as clean as I could be."

Aquillarus laughed at Gaidence.

"Of course my friend." Aquillarus collected up all the empty water canteens and with the water from one, he doubled it to fill another canteen until they were all full. Gaidence strapped them all over his shoulders, rummaged through his sack, taking a fresh set of clothing, and staggered off into the swamp to fix himself up.

Aquillarus climbed up a nearby tree to take a look to see how far away they were from the end of the swamp. He was a few branches high when he could see it clearly. The surrounding trees separated and it opened onto an empty field. Further, in the distance, he could make out the rubble of rocks and slabs of stone surrounding a tower in ruin, he could not make out anyone guarding the tower but he knew they would be there.

As he scanned the area below. He could hear Harlot waking, so he scurried back down.

"How are you feeling?" He asked, leaping to the ground.

"You'll be pleased to know it didn't kill me in the night."

"No, I guarded you fair lady to make sure it could not," Aquillarus smiled.

"Oh, how will I ever repay you," Harlot rolled her eyes.

"So today is the day," Aquillarus said and Harlot was surprised it was him who changed the subject.

"Yeah," Harlot replied, as she got up and began to pack away her things. "Where's the other one?"

"Oh he's cleaning himself up, I did him a little something, giving him enough water so he could do it properly."

"He's taken a shining to you, you make sure you watch over him for me, won't you. The Valorgrace's were such a good family to me, all I ask is you make sure nothing happens to him or his brother."

"I think I've taken a shining to him too, he's an exceptionally well mannered, brave, and striking young man. I will gladly protect him however I can, although I have only just met him, there is something about him that I cannot help but care for him. I believe with you protecting him there is not much need for my help, as I am sure that you would take care of anything that came to harm him."

"Just promise me. Whatever happens today, you take him home once it's all over. Make sure he gets home safely. The only reason I haven't made you do so already is because I know how much it means to him to try and rescue the God."

"You called him a God?"

"What? No, I didn't."

"Jenwa." Harlot looked at him strangely as it had been so long since she had been addressed by her real name, "I may not know much about you, but one thing I know is you have never referred to him as a God. I was convinced you did not believe in them, so why? It's more than revenge isn't it."

"I think you know me well enough to know I am not going to answer that question."

"You are not the only one Millerson Thact has a grudge against. I am also aware I might not see the night sky again. I act all-powerful but there is fear hidden deep down like there is in you. I owe this to the Gods. I believe they helped me escape, they forgave me for what I had done, showed me the way to go. I made them a promise if I could ever repay them or do something then I would. This is not about Millerson Thact for me, this is me returning a favor." Aquillarus just looked at Harlot waiting for her to share her story and then she did.

"He helped me. All the time. Food, clothing, flowers, tools, gifts, everything I could ever need would randomly appear at my door without warning. Some mornings when I awoke, I would just find them there. The Valorgrace's and he were the only ones who knew where I lived. He never left a note, and he never did it during the day when I was awake, always at night. I know it was him, it had to be. The last words he said to me were 'I may not be able to rid you of this evil disease but I promise I will help, protect and do what I can for you until the end comes for one of us.' This was his way."

"But still he helped you, why are you going all this way just to thank him?"

"One of the last things I said to him was, I did not believe in him. I just want him to know… I just…", she paused for a moment, changed her tone, and continued, "yeah I just want to thank him."

Harlot turned away and rummaged through her sack.

"I'm sure he already knows."

Gaidence returned with a massive grin across his face, wearing a fresh outfit. He wore a pair of black slacks, shiny black shoes, and a handmade black shirt. There was a pocket on the front of the shirt on the left breast that had three yellow stars which had been hand-stitched to it. His hair was neatly parted to the left side and his face did not have a speck of dirt on it. Harlot spotted Gaidence and instantly began to chuckle, "Oh Gade sweetheart, you're a bit adorable."

"What?" Gaidence asked blushing.

"I think she means you look very handsome. Harlot, darling, I know you wanted things to work between us but I might have had a change of heart." Aquillarus added, giving Gaidence a wink. Gaidence's already blushed. His face got an even deeper shade of red, he quickly spoke trying to cover his embarrassment from the attention.

"My mother made it. I've never worn it. She said to me before she went... away. If I ever had the opportunity to meet Avenyx, I should wear it. The symbol represents the God of Night. Each time I was in his presence, I did not have time to prepare. I wanted to wear it today for her."

"Your mother would be proud," Aquillarus added, Harlot still cackling tried to hide behind Aquillarus so Gaidence could not see her laughing.

"Ignore her, she's just jealous that she will have to use all her Temptress ways to stop them all from falling in love with you," Aquillarus said, giving him a little wink. Gaidence blushed harder and shyly began to pack the empty canteens in his sack.

"Oh, I think I'll be up for that challenge with what I have planned." Harlot said finally controlling her outbursts of laughter.

"Yes, I was waiting for this, what do you have in mind?" Aquillarus asked.

"Millerson Thact wants to call me a Temptress or Harlot. That is what I plan to give him. Gaidence is not the only one who brought a special outfit for this occasion." Harlot said as an evil grin spread across her face.

Chapter 18

Avenyx was now gagged as well as tightly bound, blood still trickled from his wound, his right cheek was shining red due to a new injury. His sour face stared across at Millerson's smirking grin.

"Now that was the fight I was expecting. Knew it was in there somewhere," Millerson grinned.

"Since these next few days may be your final ones, I would like to share a little confession, a larger reason why I hate your dear friend Ruby ever so much. Sometime shortly after you chose to put yourself in exile, or as I like to put it, you and your young mistress were driven away from the town. You disappeared almost instantly after the night of the fires, she on the other hand took a little more work. Then again she always did."

Millerson paused waiting for a reaction however Avenyx was determined now more than ever to not give him one.

"You see, Ruby had prohibited me from entering her little safe haven. This being the only place the harlot would visit and still felt safe, I knew I had to do something to get rid of her permanently. When the talks of the town about being deserted by their God or the great fires or the families that were lost stopped, I needed more. While it was just all a bit of fun to the men knowing her as Harlot the Temptress. It was the woman of the town who won this battle for me. You see men don't go home to their partner's announcing "The Temptress at the tavern kept giving me free drinks all night", why would they? It would be totally foolish. Why if they did, their partners would definitely put a stop to them going and that's not what I wanted to happen, I wanted the reverse. So as usual, on every first day of the moon when the majority of women did their trade of goods in the main street of town. I made sure a few women overheard me discussing our friend the Temptress waitress and you know very well how this town works. Let's say the very next day a few certain women paid someone a visit at Ruby's and I believe that is when she decided it was best she stayed away."

Millerson paused again and still had no reaction from Avenyx.

"Nothing to say about that? Well, the next part I know will make your blood boil. I'll give you a hint. Maybe I'll start with just a name. Ticcarus Valorgrace...."

Avenyx flinched a little, narrowed his eyes but determined not to give Millerson the reaction he wanted.

"What an unfortunate end he came to. You know after his loyal companion disappeared, he turned to the tainted ones for friendship. What a foolish mistake that was. I'll be honest it was not intentional at all, well it kind of was for good old Crusher. You remember Crusher? He was the favorite up the mountains because of his ability to smash rocks, with his fists, meaning he got more work done than the rest. He used his *'gift'* to get friends, become popular. Tried to turn people against me. Against the Town Governor. A fine example of those who are not pure using their taint to feel superior to the rest of us wouldn't you say?"

Millerson now began to start pacing back and forth across the stone floor.

"He was the first, I despised him so much. The lame jokes he would tell, that voice, the ego. The boulder was just sitting right there, above where he was working, it was *'crushing'* that it accidentally fell on him. What was more crushing was that Ticcarus Valorgrace saw it falling and rushed to push him out of the way. I think he knew it was me that pushed it, the look in his eyes as he leaped through the air towards a man double his size. Sheer terror. He knew he was not going to survive but still, he had to be the hero didn't he. It all spiraled out of control from there. The boy. When I came back for you, I came back for him also. I instructed Jacobus and his friends if they want to be part of my rebellion, they need to prove it by bringing me the youngest Valorgrace. Why? I'm glad you asked God. It was him. He saw it. No, he wasn't literally there but I got the word, the boy saw it happen in his mind. Kendall Valorgrace is tainted! Do you know what the boy did? Told his crazy mother! Before she *'took her turn for the worst'*. I like to call it went insane, she let it slip to good old Ruby too. Why does everything in that forsaken town have to run through that woman? She just has to have a finger in everyone's pie. That's right! Marni Valorgrace went running to Ruby to get you because for some zilly zolly reason she still had faith. Faith her God would come back and protect her family. What a lie that was, you couldn't even protect your closest friend because a town drove you away. Some God you turned out to be. Ruby hated me but did not believe for a second that Kendall saw me murder his father in his mind. She knew everyone knew Marni was not coping well with Ticcarus's death. It was just the words of an insane woman. It was not until a few eclipses later where Marni really went out of her mind and wandered off one day leaving her children behind to find the Gods that would bring back her husband, so the story goes. Ruby called in to pay the boys a visit, Gaidence was out and she had a chat with young Kendall Valorgrace, who shared his little secret with her. He told her secrets about herself she shared with no one, so she knew this boy was the real deal. That night she came knocking on my door with her good friend Charlie. I swear that woman will never rest until a bullet from that gun goes into my body. She told me she knew everything and was to give me a choice. If I left the town never to return, she would keep my secret. I was caught off guard, I panicked, what was I meant to do? I'll tell you what I should have done. Put that miserable woman's life to an end right there, but no I took off that very night. I swore I would come back to get my revenge on the town, the tainted, and everyone that tried to destroy me. You, my friend, made the top of my list. Oh, the Valorgrace boy is on there too and so is that tramp but you are the one that started it all, standing back watching my wife die in that fire. And who will come to your rescue? It will be the eldest Valorgrace boy as he would be so loyal and brave like his father. And a sixty-year-old floozy if she makes it through the swamps. So there you go God, you know why you're here, you know why I'm here and you know why I won't stop until I purify Thera, starting with the sleepy town of Hazy Foot."

Rage filled Avenyx's eyes, he had so much anger inside but he knew being tied down and gagged, there was not much he could do. He needed his hands to bring on the black mist to assist his escape and he needed to be able to speak to call on the powers of the night. There was one last attempt he could make but it had been so long he was not sure if anyone would be listening or cared enough to come to his aid. Avenyx closed his eyes tightly and in his mind thought hard of a place, far, far away, an island in the middle of the Great Sea that so few knew of. An island where a temple made of gold and crystallized glass sparkled in the sunlight. An island where so long ago he made an oath to aid and protect those in need no matter what he had to face. In his mind, he spoke and all he said was "By the Gods, please, I need your help." Then he waited patiently hoping that one would hear his call.

Guards, half armored in thick hide and leather helmets hid with their bows drawn or swords in hand as they watched her saunter across the empty field. Her deep purple and black gown flowed in the slight breeze, her tightly fastened corset would help her give them a distraction, while her dark hair swished back and forth with every step she took. The look would not be complete without her violet lips, constantly smiling as they stood out from the rest of her beauty-enhanced face. Every now and then she would take a glance down to make sure enough cleavage was showing and licked her teeth to maintain its shiny white appearance when she smiled. She trembled a little, trying to hold back the shakes that were coming on; another symptom of the disease she had to live with for so long. It had been a while since she had to work her magic but Harlot knew she still had it and could charm these men like it was any other night working at Ruby's Tavern. Harlot knew the layout as Aquillarus had scouted the area from high above in a tree near the edge of the swamp and prepared her. He advised Harlot there was one guard at the entrance to the tower and two hiding behind piles of rubble, there were at least another 4 in their tents and their camping area behind the tower. He said most were men but one or two were women, she assured him she could work her magic on anyone. If she could get in the tower, past the three guards out front without alarming any of the others then Aquillarus and Gaidence would take care of the rest. Harlot assured the boys she would get in and go for Avenyx, they would need to take out the small army then make their way up the tower as soon as they could. As Harlot made her way closer, the man at the door with a large sword walked across the field to meet her.

"Are you lost, ma'am?" He called out to her.

"Hello handsome, I believe I just found what I was looking for actually." She sweetly smiled at him. The guard still kept hold of his weapon but signaled for the others to stay down with his other hand.

"I'm awfully sorry ma'am but we have a bit of a situation here at the moment, I suggest you be on your way. There is an extremely dangerous man with magical abilities lurking in the swamp and I wouldn't want any harm to come to you."

Harlot was now standing directly in front of the guard who still clung to his sword tightly.

"Oh darlin, don't be apologizing to little me," she giggled and softly touched his face with the back of her hand, hesitantly he moved the sword towards her arm to try to move it away. She lowered her hand.

"Oh my, what a big sword you have there."

"I... don't want to have to use it, ma'am," he stuttered.

"Now ain't that a shame," Harlot whispered to him, giving him a seductive look.

"So what do you have in that big tower over there, I'd love for you to take me inside." she smiled sweetly.

"I really shouldn't...the man in charge...he would get very upset." He was all but trembling, he fidgeted and lowered his sword. Harlot knew this was her time to strike. She licked her lips, lowered her head to his ear, and whispered. "If you reject me I will get very upset," then licked the tip of his ear. The man instantly got goosebumps and dropped his sword.

"You promise you won't tell anyone," he nervously shot back at her.

"Would I lie to a striking young man, such as yourself?" She placed her hand on his chest in the gap where his armored vest was loosely laced together then slowly ran it down to his stomach. He took hold of her wrist.

"You have to pretend that you're my prisoner," he whispered to her, still trembling with nerves.

"Oh sweetheart, I'll pretend to be whoever you want me to be."

The man blushed bright red and turned away from her. He still kept hold of her wrist then called out loud enough so the two guards hiding could hear him. "That's right, you're not going anywhere, I'm taking you into the tower and tying you up."

"Oh darn, I've been caught," she said in a pathetic tone and gave him a little wink. Before long she was in the tower with the man closing the wooden door behind them.

I'm not sure what just happened but she's in," Aquillarus said to Gaidence as he scaled back down the tree, "are you ready?"

"I believe so," Gaidence said taking a deep breath.

"Are all the supplies hidden?"

"All hidden, except this of course." Gaidence held up Ruby's gun that he clung to so tightly.

"Are you sure you are ok? You can wait here if you like, I understand."

Gaidence shook his head vigorously.

"We stick together, only shoot if you need to. I should be able to take care of most of them and take these." Aquillarus threw Gaidence a tiny box, Gaidence struggled but caught it with his free hand and flicked it open. It contained a few matches; he looked up at Aquillarus quickly.

"Any torches, any candles you see, you light. Or if I scream out for you to light a match, you light it. I can only control an element that I can see and feel with an emotion, so to make fire I need an original source."

"Got it," Gaidence smiled back and placed the box in his breast pocket, "thank you."

"Also I want you to have this."

Aquillarus placed his hand under his robe and removed a small, shiny silver dagger.

"It was my mother's. She had Avenyx bless it for her once. I've never used it but I want you to have it in case I'm not there."

Gaidence accepted the dagger and fastened it to his belt.

"So are we just going to charge across the field?" Gaidance asked.

"No my friend, I'm going to teach you how to make an entrance. Come here and cling tightly to me."

A little unsure and with a look of confusion across his face, Gaidence walked over until he was standing directly in front of Aquillarus. He was so close he could feel his breath on the side of his face. Nervously Gaidence's eyes glanced up and met Aquillarus's who had a small smile across his face.

"I promise I won't let any harm come to you. Hold on to me." Aquillarus ordered and lifted his arms.

Gaidence strapped the gun across his back making sure it was secured tightly then wrapped both arms around Aquillarus's torso, a little frightened of what was about to happen.

"Close your eyes as you may get a little dizzy." Aquillarus smiled and Gaidence closed his eyes tightly. Aquillarus murmured some words Gaidence could not make out and suddenly felt a gust of wind began to surround them. As the wind intensified Gaidence clung tighter and suddenly it felt as if his feet were being lifted off the ground. Gaidence opened his eyes just a little to notice Aquillarus' hair and eyes were as white as a fluffy cloud. Sensing this, Aquillarus whispered, "I think you'll like this one."

Gaidence looked to the ground and could see his suspicions were correct, he was no longer standing on the ground; he was hovering just above it a little higher than the low growing shrubs.

"Give me wind!" Aquillarus called aloud, dropping his arms and wrapped them around Gaidence. Suddenly they began to spin, it was like they were in the center of a tornado. Gaidence shut his eyes tightly but he felt the gust of wind carry them out of the swamp and flew them across the field. He could feel the wind against his legs, making his pant legs flap; he could feel the spinning and began to feel a tiny bit dizzy. Then, suddenly without warning the wind stopped. Gaidence let go of Aquillarus and he crashed onto the grassy floor below.

The two guards hiding behind the rubble noticed this strange occurrence and leaped out with weapons drawn. Gaidence, still dizzy, opened his eyes and struggled to stand. Aquillarus was still floating just above the ground while both men had their arrows pointed at him. Aquillarus wasted no time as he flicked his hair, changing it from white to a dark brown color, "Stay down Gade," he called behind him, then he came crushing to the as well ground. As he did, the ground in front of him, all the way up to the tower entrance began to vigorously vibrate. The two guards staggered to find their feet also dropped their weapons and fell to the ground. One of the guards fell forward, smashing his head on a large piece of stone. Gaidence cringed a little as he witnessed this all. The mental preparation he did on the journey to this point, did not prepare him enough, and the reality of the situation had begun to kick in. It was the time; he chose to do this, he had to attempt to save the God who sacrificed himself for his brother. When the ground stopped shaking, he got to his feet, still a little dizzy but he fought it off. He slung the gun over his shoulder and held it in his hands ready as he stood courageously next to Aquillarus.

Chapter 19

"Never trust a beautiful woman," Harlot smiled, as she finished tightly binding the guard.

"You evil witch," he screamed, then spat on Harlot who instantly reacted by, slapping him across the face.

"Never spit at a woman either. It's just disgusting."

"We will one day rid this place of your kind."

With a powerful hit, Harlot clobbered him over the head, knocking him unconscious.

"Sometimes it's easier to be who they want you to be, rather than constantly proving who you really are," she said to herself shaking her head. She scanned the surroundings quickly, it was quite dim, and there were a few wooden crates in a corner and a half-open door that led to another room. Harlot knew if anyone was in there they would have come out to see what the commotion was, so she assumed Millerson would be up the top of the tower. From the memory of when Millerson used to bring her here, there was another room up the first set of stairs then the second flight of stairs, which lead up to a few different rooms. Millerson's favorite room was up the top at the back, which had a window made out of the stonewall; Harlot knew that is where he would have Avenyx. She quickly glanced around once more to double-check no one was creeping up on her then made her way up the first flight of stairs.

"Don't kill me!" The second guard called, too afraid to rise up. He was visibly horrified after watching his friend die before his eyes.

"Yet you would kill me. So I'm confused, why I should let you run free?" Aquillarus asked, taking one step at a time, slowly towards him with Gaidence following closely behind, with the gun in hand, pointing at him.

The man crawled backward trying to get away from them; he backed up until he was up against the stonewall of the tower. Aquillarus grinned, "you're not going anywhere. Gade, hold my hand, I need your help to channel an emotion." Instantly Gaidence moved closer and reached out, taking hold of Aquillarus' hand.

Aquillarus flicked his hair and his brown locks changed to green. He twisted his free hand making a circle in the air. Gaidence watched amazed as the vines that grew up the side of the broken tower began to twist and tighten around the man's hands and feet.

"Help! Get around here! He's a....a...." The man yelled out for help.

"Elementalist! They never seem to get it right," Aquillarus sighed.

Gaidence moved closer and his eyes shot up to meet with Aquillarus' vine green eyes.

"Change of plan about splitting up, go to the tower and help Harlot. I'll take care of the rest down here." Aquillarus ordered letting go of Gaidence's hand as another two guards made their way around the side of the tower.

"Are you sure?"

"Just go!" Aquillarus shouted and Gaidence took off to the entrance of the tower, "remember to light the torches."

Gaidence burst through the door into the center of the room. He was surprised to see a man bound and unconscious on the ground. He glanced at the stairs then the open door. Unsure which way to go, Gaidence froze as a familiar voice came from behind him.

"I'm not going to let you stop him. This has to be done," Jacobus shouted.

Gaidence spun around to see Jacobus closing the door behind him; Gaidence lifted the gun pointing it directly at him.

"I think we both know you're not going to shoot me with that." Gaidence raised his eyes to meet Jacobus and slowly removed the gun placing it next to him; his eyes never breaking away from Jacobus' glaze.

"Let's make it a fair fight then shall we," Gaidence said, he rolled up the sleeves of his shirt.

"Let's just finish this."

Gaidence took a strong stance as Jacobus leaped at him, he raised his fists and took a swing which Jacobus easily blocked. Jacobus retaliated with a few swift punches of his own but Gaidence dodged each of them. The two dodged blows for a little then it was Gaidence who landed the first hit, landing his fist into Jacobus's ribcage. Jacobus just smiled at him, "lucky shot." Jacobus took another swing and this time Gaidence grabbed hold of his fist and gave his arm a little twist, Jacobus grunted and ripped his arm back.

"Now that one hurt," Jacobus said, taking a few steps back then rushing forward, tackling Gaidence to the ground. The pair hit the ground with a large thud as they did. Gaidence grazed the back of his hand causing it to bleed. Jacobus managed to pin his arm down but with his free hand, Gaidence smashed it into the side of Jacobus's face, which smacked him in the nose. Instantly blood oozed out of it.

"You've broken my blasted nose!" Jacobus screamed out in pain and smashed Gaidence's hand against the ground. Gaidence now used his free hand to attempt to push the brute off him but he struggled, considering that he weighed a lot more than him. Jacobus whose face was now covered in blood, used both hands and pinned Gaidence by the shoulders. Gaidence tried to push himself free a few times but knew it was no use.

"You're not going anywhere," Jacobus spat, causing a little of his blood to spray Gaidence's face. This angered him greatly as he had tried so hard to stay clean and this was really something that annoyed him. He knew he had a way to escape but did not wish to use it. Jacobus just sat there grinning at Gaidence, not moving; knowing he wasn't going anywhere.

Gaidence took a deep breath, closed his eyes, and whispered quietly, "may the Gods forgive me." He slowly slid a hand under his back, pulling out the silver dagger, with a roar he plunged it into Jacobus' left thigh. Jacobus let out blood curling.

"Curse you! You stabbed me! He will kill your God and I will make sure he kills you too!" Jacobus screamed, tears streamed from his face. He got to his feet and limped back. He tried to pull out the dagger but the pain was too much.

"Look what you've done to me!"

Gaidence just looked him up and down, unrolled his sleeves, and wiped his face clean.

"I will do what I must," Gaidence said, leaning down to pick up the gun. As he turned his back, Jacobus used all his strength to leap forward to get one last attack at Gaidence. At that moment a black raven flew in from the doorway leading off to the other room screeching loudly. The raven was heading directly into Jacobus' face. Gaidence spun around and staggered backward as he watched the display before his eyes. Jacobus was swinging his arms trying to land a hit on the raven as the bird continued to claw at his face. Jacobus managed to get a clean hit, sending it squawking and colliding into the wall. The bird flapped around a little then fell lifeless to the ground. Gaidence looked at Jacobus' blood-covered face. His nose was almost now double the size. He had large, deep scratches all over his face. One was over his left eye, which Jacobus closed tightly, knowing serious damage had been done. Jacobus raised one hand to his bloody face as he crouched, trying to retrieve the dagger from his thigh with the other.

"You killed Eventide!" Gaidence roared, "that was Avenyx's raven!"

Gaidence still had the gun in his hand. Without thinking, he held it tightly but instead of pointing toward Jacobus, he held it the other way round. With the larger end of the gun, he swung it, cracking Jacobus in the side of the head. Instantly Jacobus fell in a heap to the floor.

Gaidence stood for a moment, tears welled up in his eyes but he was not going to cry, he mustn't, he agreed to do whatever it took and he was not going to give up now. He took a deep breath, walked over to Jacobus and ripped out the dagger from his leg then returned it to his belt behind his back. He walked over to the raven that had not survived the collision with the wall.

"I'm sorry dear friend. May the Gods watch over you wherever it is you now rest."

Gaidence sensed someone behind him, fearing Jacobus had awoken, his body tensed but then he heard a voice. The soft voice of a woman.

"Oh, beautiful creature. May you live to fight another day," she whispered. Instantly, Gaidence spun around but there was no one there. When he returned to Eventide the raven had burst into flames. His eyes widened, fixed on the flames when the loud caw of the raven filled the room. From the flames, a smaller raven emerged and flew from the room. The flames diminish and Gaidence sat puzzled, but he knew there was no time for questions, he needed to find Harlot and more importantly Avenyx.

He looked at the stairs noticing unlit torches lining the wall heading up. He raced over to the first, lighting as instructed then suddenly from up above at the top of the tower he heard someone scream in pain and he raced up the stairs.

Harlot slowly approached the wooden door, she could hear Millerson's voice booming on the other side. This was it. For so long she had waited to face both these men once again, now she got the chance to do it. She made sure one dagger was secured tightly by her belt behind her back and she had the other firmly held in her hand. She quickly fixed her hair a little, tightened her corset until she could barely breathe, and adjusted her bust. Harlot grinned to herself, then with a mighty kick, she burst through the door.

Millerson froze mid-sentence, picked up a one-handed ax that lay on the table and raised it above his head.

"Hope I'm not interrupting," She grinned. Her grin did not last long as soon as she spotted Avenyx tied, gagged, and injured to a chair. Sadness filled her eyes, he looked at her and shook his head. She could read the expression on his face. Why?

"I must say I'm a little surprised to see you, but not at all disappointed," Millerson said.

"Expecting someone else?" She asked.

"Well, honestly I knew the old bat wouldn't come trenching through the swamp herself. But I didn't think she would track down a lady of the night to do her dirty work. Where did she find you anyway, I thought I got rid of you a long time ago?"

"The same could be said about you. You've aged terribly Millerson. All those crazy notions in your head finally took its toll it seems. Avey, on the other hand, you haven't aged a day."

There was silence for a moment, the trio just stared at one another. Neither Harlot nor Millerson made any sudden moves. It had been years since Millerson had seen Harlot, he wasn't prepared to see her ever again. Being in the tower brought up feelings he had long forgotten and wished they'd never resurfaced.

"So what are you going to do? We both know you are no Temptress so there is no point attempting to put me under some spell."

"Who says I'm not a Temptress, I mean it's been a while since I've been told otherwise. For the record, I don't need a spell when I have this." Harlot quickly threw her dagger from her hand in Millerson's direction which he dodged and she watched it clang against the stone floor.

"You missed," Millerson smiled. Avenyx looked at Harlot, his grey eyes filled with disapproval. He took a deep breath, closed his eyes, and when he opened them again they were black as night. Harlot knew he was up to something, so she knew she had to draw Millerson's attention away from Avenyx, although Harlot did not need Avenyx's help for what she had planned, as it was far more what Millerson deserved.

"Oh Millerson, I don't want you to die just yet, you know how much I can never say goodbye without one last kiss," Harlot said in her most sultry voice.

"Why? Has it been a while, since no man would come near you and all the women must hate you."

"Let's not bring up the past. I mean we're together again in our secret spot, isn't that the main thing."

"I'm no fool. You've come for him. I may have driven you both out of the town but I'm sure you still kept seeing each other. You were so close that night when I found you, you were practically in each other's arms. You both got what you deserved."

"You made me feel so unwanted, so worthless. People hated me. We never were with each other. I was always alone for so long!" Harlot screamed with tears in her eyes. For so long she had waited for this moment. She knew what she had to do, she was a few feet away from Millerson, the man she despised most. She slowly took a step forward. Still, with one hand behind her back, she held a dagger by the blade. As she tightened her grip, the blade cut open her skin, and the black blood that filled her body began to ooze out.

"May I remind you, my dear Harlot, I have an ax in my hand," Millerson said calmly. Avenyx couldn't do anything but watch the events play out before his black eyes. As it did, through the window, the darkness of night began to roll in, even though it was the middle of the day.

"Don't you want one last kiss? For old time's sake, before you get rid of me once and for all? I mean that is your plan, to get rid of me so no one knows the truth that Millerson Thact lied and really was in love with the Temptress," Harlot said. She had gotten so close to him now that she could see the tiny details of his face.

Millerson looked deep into her eyes, such beauty he thought. He knew he couldn't resist one last kiss. He leaned in and passionately kissed Harlot on the lips. As he did, Harlot flicked the dagger she concealed behind her back and drove it into Millerson's right forearm causing him to instantly drop the ax.

"Arghhh!" He screamed out in rage. With his left arm, he went to take a swing at Harlot which she blocked then with her oozing hand she took hold of Millerson's wound squeezing it tightly. She watched on with a grin as Millerson's deep red blood mixed with her black as night blood. She raised her head to face him and said, "Sometimes you need to feel worthless to know your true value."

Millerson looked down at his arm and realized what was happening.

"You evil Temptress! You Harlot!" He called as he shoved her away.

"Destined to die they call it. It gets worse over time. You will have to live with the pain until one day it consumes you and takes your life. Great fevers, cold sweats, blackouts, headaches, dizziness. The list goes on. So tell me Millerson Thact, who's tainted now?" Harlot asked.

She staggered backward. Her head started to fill with pain and the dizziness began to set in. She knew these symptoms too well, something she fought and put up with for far, far too long. She knew it had gotten worse since she began this foolish trek to save a God. Harlot stood so she was facing both Avenyx and Millerson and rose her dagger. Millerson reached down for his ax and Avenyx began to struggle with trying to free himself from out the window. Harlot could see it now appeared to be night. The room was dark however, a burning torch gave off enough light for them to clearly see one another.

Harlot took one last look at the monster Millerson that became then turned to Avenyx and whispered the words "Nothing will ever defeat me." Tears began to stream down Harlot's face and with a mighty shout she yelled 'BY THE GODS!' With her right hand, she plunged the dagger into her own chest then dropped to the floor. Both men watch on in disbelief as the black blood gushed out, leaving her body. With a mighty thrash, Avenyx filled with so much emotion, anger, rage, pain, sadness, spite and he managed to break an arm free from the ropes and chains.

"This was you! You..." was all Millerson could say looking at the God. Tears streamed down Avenyx's face. Millerson aimed the ax towards Avenyx and took a step forward.

"This ends now!" He called.

"Yes, it does!" Gaidence called from the doorway with Charlie pointed at Millerson.

Chapter 20

Gaidence looked down at Harlot's lifeless body on the floor. Tears welled up in his eyes.

"May the Gods forgive you!" he yelled, taking a step forward.

"You are mistaken, boy. Stay out of this, it does not concern you," Millerson shot back.

"For my brother. For my mother. For my father. FOR THE GODS!" Gaidence screamed as he slowly pulled the trigger on Ruby's gun.

What happened next all seemed to happen slowly for Gaidence, as time almost came to a standstill. When he pulled the trigger and the bullet left the gun, Millerson flung his ax, and at the same time, Avenyx flicked his hand across in front of him. The first thing Gaidence noticed was the black mist around Millerson's feet, the same black mist that appeared in the alley the night Gaidence was chased and when he first encountered Avenyx. The next thing he saw was the bullet piercing Millerson's shoulder causing black blood to spurt out. The mist then picked up Millerson and flung him across the room and he flew out the window. Gaidence was unsure if the bullet had killed Millerson and hoped if it didn't, the fall would. Before it seemed as if time started to catch up with itself, the last thing Gaidence noticed was the ax that was wedged in Avenyx's chest with a large amount of blood pouring from the wound.

"No! NO! NO!" Gaidence screamed, dropping the gun to the floor and rushed over to Avenyx. Instantly he took the gag from Avenyx's mouth and began to clear the ropes and chains off the God.

"Gaidence Valorgrace..." Avenyx's voice was croaky, he coughed as he spoke and blood spat out of his mouth.

"You can't die. You mustn't! I've come to rescue you. Please." Gaidence was unsure what to do. He leaned forward, arms stretched out to grab the ax, he planned to remove it but feared it would kill him instantly. Avenyx reached out his hand and took hold of Gaidence's.

"I am ready. Do not blame yourself. You needed to be here."

"Avenyx I do not understand, you are a God."

"And have been for a long time. And I am sure I still will be."

"But..."

"Promise me the Valorgrace name lives on."

"Please, what can I do?"

"Nothing. My time has come." Avenyx spluttered again and more blood came out of his mouth and his wound gushed faster.

"There must be something," Gaidence screamed and slammed his fist against the back of the chair.

"There is... If Millerson lives he won't give up. I could not let you take his life, this is not your fight. Help them. Your brother. All of them. And the Gods and Goddesses, seek them out. Thera doesn't need purifying. If it is a war these people want... be ready."

"Avenyx..."

"And tell Ruby..." Avenyx coughed again and his eyes flickered.

"Don't you die!"

He opened his eyes again.

"Tell Ruby. As long as night comes, wherever I go I'll be thinking of her."

"I promise, I will."

With his free hand, Gaidence made a fist, raised it to his chest, he could feel the symbols stitched into his shirt.

Between the tears, he softly whispered "By the Gods." And Avenyx whispered these words back to him.

Avenyx closed his eyes and Gaidence watched in the dimness of the dark room as the God's life left his body.

Gaidence let go of Avenyx's hand as he was startled by a bright light that appeared from behind him. He turned, and before him was a tall and elegant blonde woman dressed in a tight silk white gown. She walked up to Avenyx ignoring Gaidence, acting like he wasn't even there and she took hold of his hand.

"It's time I take you home, brother. Your end is finally here, which will bring the beginning. The death of the first God, this day will be remembered," she whispered, her voice was so soft Gaidence barely could hear it. But he recognized it, it was the same voice from behind him at the base of the tower, with Eventide. Her hand began to glow then, so did Avenyx's and then the glowing covered his whole body.

"Stop! What is happening? Who are you?" Gaidence called to her.

She turned to face Gaidence and spoke, "When the first of them fall, a Valorgrace shall stand to see. When the last is awoken, a Valorgrace shall be the one to set her free." Gaidence did not totally understand what she meant and began to repeat this riddle in his head.

The woman stretched out her hand and pointed it towards Gaidence and he fell instantly to the floor, unconscious.

"Get up Gade!" Aquillarus called. Gaidence opened his eyes. He could see Aquillarus's fiery red eyes looking back at him, he then noticed a small fireball spinning in his hand. Still, a little groggy Gaidence looked over to Harlot's body then to the empty chair where the God once was.

"We don't have time. There was more than I expected, you'll have to explain what happened to Harlot later. Where is the God so we can get out of here?"

"He's gone."

"What do you mean gone? Talk fast because they will be on us at any moment."

"He's dead. Millerson killed him and then..."

"What? We failed!"

"I think it was meant to happen. Kendall said it would and it did. I think I was meant to be here. I think this is the start of something very bad."

"I'll say. A man killed a God. Once word gets out who knows what will happen. I mean, what will the Gods do? And if Millerson has more followers this will make them feel empowered."

"I don't know."

The sound of footsteps came from outside the door coming up the stairs.

"Stand by the window, we're using wind to get out of here," Aquillarus ordered and Gaidence raced to the window, he looked down in the darkness at the field below although it was hard to see, he was certain that Millerson was no longer down there.

"Sorry my dear, I wish I could take you with us and give you a proper burial as you deserve," Aquillarus said looking at Harlot's body, he then bent down and kissed her softly on the forehead, "thank you. For more than you'll ever know."

Aquillarus got to his feet, murmured some words. The fireball doubled in size and he flung it at the doorway. He then raced over to Gaidence, wrapped his arms around him, and leaped out the window. As they fell, they were swept up by a gust of wind and carried safely to the edge of the Swamp. They hit the ground with a thud then raced into the swamp puffing and panting for air. Once they made it far enough to not be seen, they turned back and watched the tower burn in flames.

Once the boys caught their breath, Aquillarus searched in the darkness for their hidden supplies to light a lantern.

"I'm sorry," Gaidence whispered.

"For what?" Aquillarus asked.

"I couldn't save him. If I had killed Millerson straight away before he got to Harlot. Before he could throw that ax at Avenyx. I know now it was all meant to be but… It just doesn't feel right."

Aquillarus came back over to Gaidence and placed his hand on his shoulder.

"You did what you could. We all did. One thing I have learned is that things do not always end out the way we want them to but something else usually comes along. Avenyx was just one God of many. I loved and worshiped him, I am certain I and many others will mourn his passing. However, I'm sure there are others out there, others that we have yet to know, who will watch over and protect us until our or their end comes."

Now I have left the world known as Thera, passed on, on my way to a greater place. I still have questions, questions that I struggled to find an answer to. I still wonder how does one get their title? Is it something we earn by doing a heroic deed? Something we are born with and destined to grow into? Something we strive towards or do whatever it takes to have and be proud of? Or is it none of those reasons at all? Just something, someone decides to call us until it eventually catches on, and this who we become? Whether a God, a Harlot, an Elementalist, a Purist, or just a little boy with the gift to see the future. We are each individually different, so what is it that makes four of these tainted and one not. Why should it be the decision of any other being to make that call?

In my time, and a very long time it was, the only title I tried to live up to was my own, Avenyx. No matter what others called me, I promised myself I would always be Avenyx and the only person I needed to prove this to was myself. Was I a great God to the people of Thera? This is something I do not know, as I was not trying to be. Did I favor the gifted and act all tainted as accused? I believe not. I am Avenyx. Although my time has finally come and death has taken me, I'll still be known as the God of Night for some time after. To the only person that matters, I am simply me and no title or label is going to change that.

Made in the USA
Middletown, DE
29 April 2022

64936091R00146